A STRANGER ARRIVES
THIS CHRISTMAS

CP WARD

In Memory of Her Royal Highness,
Her Majesty The Queen

Thank you for your service

A STRANGER ARRIVES THIS CHRISTMAS

PART I

OPEN FOR THE HOLIDAYS

1

FRUSTRATING PERSISTENCE

'I'M SORRY, COULD YOU JUST WAIT A SECOND—'

The man in the woolly hat shook his head, balled his fists and banged them on the countertop.

'No, no, no. If I wait much longer I'll be dead. If you'd answer your stupid phones I wouldn't have to show up here in the first place.'

Annie Collins, a phone pressed against her ear as an old lady coughed and began to repeat her account number for the fourth time, could only give a grim smile at the irony of it all.

'I'll be with you in a moment,' she said to the man, while trying to type the woman's number into a computer. As she pressed a seven instead of a six and then lost her concentration, she silently cursed. 'I'm afraid we're a little short staffed today. Someone called in sick—'

'Let me guess, a little sniffle? I bet if I open their MySpace I'll see pictures of Thorpe Park—'

'Could you repeat that again?' Annie said to the woman on the phone, wondering at the same time who still used MySpace. 'Sir, I'll be right with you.'

'That's the third time you've said that. Where's your manager? No doubt it's some little whippersnapper who hasn't even had a shave yet. Well, I've got a few strips to tear off him. Hey, you over there!'

'Sir, please!' Annie said, standing up, wishing she could catch the eye of the security guard, but he was outside the main doors, chuckling as he peered at his phone.

'I'd prefer it if you called me madam,' came a voice from the phone. 'I know you young people are all confused these days, but I'm a bit more traditional.'

'I'm sorry, Madam,' Annie said, a little too loudly.

'I'll climb over there and drag him out myself,' said the man in the woolly hat, leaning on the countertop as he tried to get one leg up, knocking a box of pens on to the floor.

'Sir, no!'

'No, really, I prefer madam.'

Annie put the phone receiver down. Someone else had pressed the alarm, and now Geoff the security guard came running back in through the door as the man tried to lever himself up, managing to get one hand over the top of the glass screen as his legs dangled off the edge of the countertop. As Geoff reached him, the man let go and slid down to the floor. He let out a sudden gasp then twisted around, hands over his heart, a look of horror on his face.

'I think I'm having a heart attack,' he groaned.

'Ambulance!' Geoff shouted, loud enough to give someone else a heart attack, as the man in the woolly hat fixed Annie with a stare that seemed to say, *this is your fault.*

Annie could only stare dumbstruck as chaos began to ensue, alarms blaring, people running back and forth, screaming and shouting and not staying calm in any way whatsoever. Feeling caught in the eye of an impromptu banking maelstrom, she lifted the phone to her ear, only to hear the old lady snap, 'Your name is Annie Collins, isn't it? I'm just checking because I'd like to make a complaint….'

~

A scattering of circulars on her mat seemed to have been put there merely to trip her. Annie kicked them aside as she went into her pokey bedsit and sat down on the bed. It was only six o'clock but if she fell asleep now she might get a few decent hours before the police sirens woke her up. It didn't help that her only window didn't quite shut properly, but Friday nights were always the worst, even if at least tomorrow was Saturday, meaning she didn't have to go into work.

As she lay on the bed, however, all she could think about was the look of horror in the eyes of the man with the woolly hat as he clutched his heart. She'd hoped he was faking it to punish her inattentiveness, but he had still been staring with a wild look in his eyes when the ambulance pulled up outside and the paramedics rushed in to aid him.

According to her boss, who had been in touch with the hospital, he had been stabilised and would make a complete recovery, but Annie still felt bad, as though it had somehow been her fault.

With a sigh, she stood up and went to her little kitchenette, noticing to her frustration that the fridge door had failed to close properly again, meaning her milk had likely gone off. She closed it with an angry jerk of her knee, which in turn knocked one of the magnets and the postcard it was holding loose.

It was from her cousin Maggie, currently enjoying a honeymoon in the south of France with Henry, her perfect new husband. Annie had met him only once, a few months ago during one of Maggie's rare trips south from her new home in Scotland to visit some family. Annie had been somewhat overawed by Henry—much preferring him to Maggie's previous boyfriend, Dirk, who had practically dripped with slime and been underhand enough to ask for Annie's phone number while Maggie was in the toilet at a family New Year's gathering—but all his apparent perfectness had been easier to temper with the fact that he was a reindeer farmer. As far as Annie was concerned, it was long overdue that Father Christmas got with the times and bought himself a more modern sleigh, perhaps one made by Tesla that ran off batteries or solar panels. In time, perhaps, Rudolph and his smelly chums would be relegated to a Christmas afterthought.

There was nothing in the fridge to eat except some leftover curry, which was probably a little warm now to be safe. It looked like chips again, for the third night this week. Still, mushy peas counted as a vegetable, didn't they?

She went to the door and reached up to take her thickest jacket down off the hook. The nearest chippy was a ten minute walk, and the weather had closed in over the afternoon, bringing with it a chilly November wind.

As she went to slip it over her arm, she dropped it on the floor. Bending to pick it up, she found herself scooping up a handful of letters at the same time, and turned to toss them into a basket she kept by the door which once a week she emptied into a recycling bin outside work.

She frowned at one that looked official, then realised it was the same scamming law firm as before. The one that claimed she had inherited a manor house in the Lake District.

The first one, addressed to her old married name, which had shown up in the second week of September, had made her smile. She had read it all the way through, wondering when the hit was going to come, the "we only need you to send us five thousand pounds and we can release the deeds to you" bit. Instead, there was just a phone number, asking her to contact them, because they had further details. She had ignored it, of course, and tossed the letter into the recycling basket, hoping it ended up part of a decent roll of toilet paper.

The second letter had been pretty much a repeat of the first. This time she had tossed it straight into the bin and felt a little guilty about it later.

It had been another long day at work, made worse by spotting a guy during her lunch hour who looked a little like Troy.

It wasn't him, of course, but it had been a bit of a shock.

According to his Facebook, which Annie would usually stalk after a couple of glasses of wine, he was living in Malaga with a beautiful young Spanish wife, enjoying easy days on the beach and cool, wine bar evenings. Probably there would soon be a child on the way—something Annie had never been able to give him during their five years of marriage—and their life would be seven shades of perfect.

There was no way whatsoever he would be wandering around the Exeter shops on a Tuesday afternoon, but nevertheless his doppelganger had ruined Annie's day, even before the crazy guy and his heart attack had put a big fat cherry on the top.

'Sod it,' she muttered, putting her coat back on the hook and taking the letter over to the kitchen, where she found a packet of supermarket own-brand custard creams in a cupboard and the remains of a bottle of wine warming in the fridge. 'Let's be a princess.'

She sat down on her IKEA recliner, stuffed a biscuit

into her mouth, and opened the letter, cringing as she always did at the sight of her old married name:

Dear Mrs. Annie Weathersby,

Would you please get in touch with us at Barnsley and Sons Solicitors at your earliest opportunity? Your grandfather's estate needs to be executed.

'So do I,' Annie said, taking a large slug of wine, then immediately breaking into a fit of coughing as a piece of the biscuit she was still chewing went down the wrong way.

You have been assigned as the sole beneficiary of your grandfather's will, and it is your responsibility to take ownership of it. Should you then decide to sell or lease the land and its property, we can be of assistance with that.

'I bet you can,' Annie said. 'How much?'

In addition, your grandfather employed several members of staff, the ongoing status of which needs to be established—

'And for that we'll need your credit card number,' Annie said, rolling her eyes, preparing to rip the paper in two. After all, it was a load of rubbish. Her grandparents on both sides were long dead.

—so please get in touch at your earliest convenience and we can discuss the transferring of the deeds into your name.

'I bet you can,' Annie muttered, stuffing another biscuit into her mouth and spitting crumbs all over the floor.

Lastly, and on a personal note, I would like to congratulate you. Your grandfather was a customer of our company for many years, and we look forward to serving you in the future, and helping to meet the ongoing needs of Stone Spire Hall and its Estate.

The letter was signed by someone called Barbara Beddingfield. Annie held it up to the light, looking for little indentations in the paper to prove it had been written by a real human with a pen, rather than printed off a computer.

It certainly looked like it, but what did it matter? It was still a scam.

She screwed it up and tossed it over her shoulder, then looked out of her second floor window at the side wall of the neighbouring building.

She smiled. She quite fancied being a lady of the manor. Wouldn't it be nice to live in a big mansion with fields and gardens and orchards?

Wishful thinking. She was Annie Collins, formerly Weathersby, thirty-seven, divorced, a bedsit-living bank clerk with no car, boyfriend, or future. But Christmas was coming, after all. Perhaps she'd find a handsome prince in her stocking. Knowing her luck, however, he would probably be on the run from the police, his costume stolen from the bargain rail in TK Maxx.

She realised she had already finished what was left of the wine, so got up to check in the cupboard beside the sink to see if there was another stray bottle hiding at the back. Alas, the cupboard was bare. She would need to make a run to the corner shop if she wanted to get obliterated, but it had just started to rain.

Her phone was lying on the floor underneath the chair. When she reached down to pick it up, however, she found a lump of screwed up paper sitting on top of it.

The letter.

It must have bounced off the wall. With a smile, she wondered if it was a sign.

She picked up the crumpled ball, smoothed it out on her lap, and dialed the number before she could chicken out. Only as she did so did she remember it was nearly seven p.m. on a Friday night, and any kind of law firm would surely be closed.

She was about to hang up when a woman's voice said, 'Hello?'

'Ah, hello … this is Annie Collins. I'm just calling you because you sent me a letter—'

'Annie Collins? I don't know—'

'It, ah, used to be Annie Weathersby, but I go by Collins these days.'

'Miss Collins, I do apologise. So, about your inheritance … if we could just confirm your identification—'

Annie rolled her eyes. 'Okay, so I need to send you a copy of my passport, is that right? And I suppose you need my bank account number? Sure, don't worry, I'll put them in an envelope with a key to my flat. Although I'm not sure what you could do with that.'

'Miss Collins—'

Annie ended the call and let out a long sigh. A scam, as she had thought. Well, it had been too good to be true, which, of course, meant it couldn't be true.

Her phone was buzzing in her hand, Barbara Beddingfield's number flashing up. Annie declined the call, put her phone on the countertop, then got up to find her umbrella. Sometimes it was best to dream small, and finding another glass of wine in her hand was a good enough dream for a rainy Friday night.

A RAY OF SUNSHINE

JULIE GOODMAN WAS WAITING ON A BENCH IN Cathedral Green when Annie arrived, holding two coffees from the garage around the corner. At the sight of her best friend with a blanket over her knees as she rubbed her hands together, Annie felt a pang of guilt that she'd not at least invited her to the Starbucks on the high street … but money was tight. Her electric bill had arrived that morning. The fridge which hadn't been working properly anyway was now permanently unplugged, and she had gone so far as to sit in the public library this morning to charge her phone.

'I was just wondering if you'd stood me up,' Julie said, smiling as Annie sat down. 'You could have come round to mine, you know. Darren's taken the kids to the new soft play on the industrial estate.'

'Sorry, I didn't think to ask.'

Julie smiled. 'And I'm not scared of your place. I have been there, remember?'

'I'll get something bigger.' Annie shrugged. 'One day.' She grinned. 'Maybe even two whole rooms.'

Julie took one of the cups and they touched them together. 'Well, cheers. Look at us, party animals.'

'We could just pretend we've come from an all night rave.'

'Sounds great. I'll dance on the bench while you sleep underneath it.'

'Just like old times?'

'Something like that.'

They lapsed into an easy but slightly nostalgic silence. While they shared the same age—their birthdays were just two days apart—these days they shared little else. While Julie, whom Annie had first met in a house share at Exeter University, had married a computer analyst with whom she'd since had three children, Annie's long, drawn out divorce had left her on the verge of poverty.

'So, you said you had a weird phone call? It wasn't Troy playing games, was it?'

Annie hadn't considered it, but now that she did, it didn't seem like Troy's style. He had taken everything from her in the divorce, dragging out proceedings until most of Annie's share of their house sale had gone on lawyer's fees. After ensuring that Annie was left destitute, he had swanned off to sunny Spain, married a beautiful local, and no doubt now lived easily off an online consultancy business. Annie, alone and broke, now struggled to make ends meet from her bank job, any chances of promotion curtailed by frequent, harrowing court dates.

'I'm pretty sure Troy's done with me,' Annie said at last. 'I mean, I've not had a single email or phone call in over a year. Now that he's reduced me to a barely functioning shell, I don't think he has any more use for me.'

'Well, that's a good thing, isn't it? You can start to rebuild. How's work?'

Annie sighed. 'I'm on a disciplinary. Some nutter tried to attack me, and apparently I didn't follow correct procedure. Something like that. To be honest, I don't really care. Maybe I'll look for something else.'

'With your experience, I imagine there are lots of bank jobs available.'

'Bank jobs....' Annie sighed again. 'Sometimes I wish I'd been more ambitious. You know, trained to be an astronaut or an explorer or something.'

Julie chuckled. 'It's not too late. You're still young.'

'Thirty-seven's not young. You get grandmas my age these days.'

'But look on the bright side. You're single, you don't have any kids, and you haven't filled out the way that happens when you have three of them.' Julie held up her arms. 'I mean, look at me. At least I don't have to worry about getting cold in the winter.'

'But you *glow*. I'm like an unwanted doll stuck at the back of the shelf.'

'Let me just go and get my paint brush so I can paint the sky grey.'

Annie looked up. 'It's already grey.'

'Greyer.'

'I'm sorry, I didn't mean to be all doom and gloom. Why don't we walk up the high street and look through some shop windows?'

Julie patted Annie on the knee. 'Come on, let's cheer you up. It's nearly Christmas, isn't it?'

'Yep. That wonderful time of year best remembered for when I found a present under the tree addressed to one of Troy's floozies. Of course he tried to argue that he had an Aunt Charlene I'd previously never heard of, and that for some reason he was giving her a pearl necklace, but whatever—'

'Stop!'

Annie clamped her mouth shut. 'Sorry—'

'Don't even say that. From now on, we only say positive things. Okay?'

Afraid she'd say something negative out of habit, Annie just nodded.

'What's going on in your life that's good?'

Annie frowned. The fridge was disconnected, her landlord was refusing to fix the window that didn't shut properly, and she had scuffed her best pair of shoes on a corner of pavement while running for a bus last week. She was worried she had IBS after living off chips, coffee and cheap wine for the last month, and she was one black mark away from possibly losing her job—

'I'm waiting. One thing.'

'I … I … inherited a manor house.'

Julie burst into laughter and rocked backwards, nearly falling off the bench.

'I knew it was there. Your sense of humour. I couldn't believe it had completely disappeared.'

'No, really. This law firm in the Lake District keeps hassling me. Apparently my grandfather left me a country estate.'

'Are you serious? That's awesome.'

'I doubt it's real, but we're being positive now, aren't we? They haven't actually asked for money, but they do want proof of my identity. It's bound to be one of those 419 scams, though, isn't it?'

'Perhaps your grandfather was secretly rich.'

'And secretly alive? I've always been told he died more than twenty years ago.'

'Oh.'

Annie spread her arms. 'See? Impossible.'

'But what if he didn't? What if he just told your

parents he was dead, but he was actually still alive, and totally rich?'

'"Hey guys, pretend I'm dead, then in twenty-odd years I'll come back and leave a country estate to your daughter".' Annie shrugged. 'Sure. I suppose it's not totally impossible.'

'Have you asked your mother?'

Annie frowned. Her father was dead fifteen years, and her mother, who had met a Canadian tourist on a train a couple of years later, was now happily remarried and living in Vancouver.

'I haven't,' she said. 'I don't know how I'd bring it up. Dad's death was hard on her, but she's so blissfully happy now that I wouldn't want to ruin it by trying to dig up the past.'

'In that case, you might as well go and take a look.'

'What … you mean—'

'Get on a train, go up to the Lake District, and have a look.'

'But what if—'

'Don't give them any money, but wouldn't it be worth the cost of a train ticket just to find out? Plus you could have a bit of a holiday at the same time.'

'I can't afford it—'

'Don't worry, if you go off-peak it's cheaper, and if you're really desperate, Benjamin's got a two-man tent he uses for scouts. I'm sure he wouldn't mind if I lent it to you.'

'I suppose I could empty out my change jar, and I have loads of holiday I can take, because I can never afford to go anywhere.'

'That's the spirit. And I tell you what, if it does turn out to be for real, and not just a barn in the corner of a field, me, Darren and the kids will all come up for

Christmas.' Julie chuckled. 'I'll make sure they address you as Baroness.'

Annie glanced up at the sky, just as the sun unexpectedly broke through the wall of cloud, briefly bathing them in sunshine.

'Um, thanks. But it's probably just a barn in a field.'

'Then you won't have any need for Benjamin's tent, will you?'

3

A LITTLE FRIGHT

BARBARA BEDDINGFIELD TAPPED ON THE STEERING wheel, nodded at a crooked sign at the end of a narrow drive leading off into a grassy valley, and said in a cheerful voice, 'Ah, here we are.'

Annie frowned as Barbara pulled the car into the roadside and switched off the engine.

'Here? Are you sure? I can't see anything except fields.' She smiled. 'Those sheep over there have faces like teddy bears.'

Barbara chuckled. 'They're Herdwick,' she said. 'Apparently Beatrix Potter loved them.'

'That's nice and everything … but are you sure this is the place?'

'Yes, yes. It's just down there.'

'But … that road just disappears.'

'It's actually a private driveway. And you know how people are. They like to be secretive. Your grandfather too, no doubt. The house is just down behind that fell—that's what we call hills round here, by the way—in the valley. You'll see it as soon as you go around the corner.'

'Can't we drive down there?'

Barbara shook her head. 'I'm afraid not. The grate's got a hole in it, hasn't it?' She nodded at the cattle grid between the corners of stone wall at the drive's entrance. Indeed, a bar appeared to be missing, leaving a worrying gap. Whether a car could still get across or not was anyone's guess, but Barbara didn't appear willing to take the chance.

'So, we're walking from here?'

'You, dear. I'm afraid I have another client to meet. But just call me and I'll pick you up, take you back to the station in Quimbeck if you need to.'

Annie held up her phone. 'I've not had a signal since we left the village.'

'Ah, but the house will have a phone, won't it?'

'Will it?'

'Of course, dear. Aren't you excited?'

Annie gave half a shrug. 'I'd say scared was a better description.'

'Don't worry, Mrs. Growell will be waiting for you. She knows to expect you.'

'Mrs. … Growl?'

'That's right, dear. Mrs. Growell.' Barbara gave a slightly tense sigh and tapped the steering wheel with the palms of both hands, as though keen to get on with the rest of her day. 'Right, are you ready?'

'I suppose so.'

'Good luck, dear. Terribly exciting, isn't it? It's such a joy to be involved with this. It's not every day that someone inherits a manor house, is it?' She gave a little chuckle that sounded so manufactured Annie could have bought it in a toy shop. 'Are you ready to go and claim your destiny?'

This time Annie couldn't resist the hint and climbed out of the car. Barbara gave her a brief wave and sped off up the road. Annie watched the little red car as it meandered out of sight along the narrow road lined on either side by quaint stone walls, thinking how it reminded her of the opening sequence to Postman Pat. She began to whistle the theme tune as she made a slow circle, the sound fading on her lips as the enormity of the landscape quite literally took her breath away. Rolling fells and open moorland surrounded her on all sides. In the valley, a lake glittered. In fact, she felt like she could see every corner of the world, except the one that now belonged to her, tucked away out of sight at the end of the gravel drive stretching off into the valley.

Beside the cattle grid, the leaning sign that greeted her was something of an oxymoron:

Welcome to Stone Spire Hall
PRIVATE PROPERTY
STAY OUT
(unless invited in)

Annie shouldered her small rucksack, having left everything else in a locker in Quimbeck's tiny train station, and stepped carefully over the hole in the cattle grid, hoping that this property left to her by her grandfather actually proved to exist.

Stone Spire Hall.

It certainly had a mystical—and slightly awkward— ring to it. In the absence of any kind of photographic proof, her imagination had begun to run wild, creating it at once as a magnificent National Trust manor house, then five minutes later as a tumbledown barn, holes in the roof, bats, everything.

What she couldn't seem to do was see it as something in the middle, but as she started down the drive, the lake glittering in the distance, she figured that within a matter of minutes she would find out.

Like a Christmas ribbon, the drive slowly uncurled as she descended into the valley, yet like a frustrating pass-the-parcel at a giant children's party it refused to show her too much at a time. The moorland gradually gave way to scraggly, wind-hassled trees, which grew larger and larger until she found herself walking in a quiet pine forest, the lake no longer in sight, and only the occasional cry of a heron or lost seagull reassuring her that she hadn't walked through some kind of portal into an entirely different world. The road narrowed until she doubted a car would even fit, the trees pressing in on what had become little more than a potholed, puddly lane.

As she came to another corner, arcing away to the left, she paused for a moment, breathing in the scent of the pine forest, feeling the November chill on her face. As she looked into the trees she wondered if she ought to feel scared, but everything felt so peaceful and calm. As she looked around at the trees, she wondered how they might look with Christmas lights hanging through their branches.

And then, to her sudden horror, back in the shadows beneath the dark green canopy, something moved.

Annie let out a sharp gasp, but for a few seconds she was rooted to the spot, unable to move. Then, as something large and antlered stepped out of a thicket of undergrowth into the space between two lines of trees, turned, gave a snort and began to walk in her direction, she managed to find the will to move. At first just walking quickly, then when the beast showed no sign of slowing down or running off, she began to move a little quicker, until she was jogging down the drive, her rucksack bouncing against her shoulder, the strap constantly slipping as she tried to look back.

Behind her, the reindeer stepped out of the trees and turned to face her.

Society's goodwill towards such beasts meant that a sliver of sanity told Annie not to be afraid, but all she felt was a deep, primal horror. Those antlers would toss her twenty feet through the air, its hooves would trample her, and no doubt it had some kind of teeth that would rip her to shreds, and probably eat her. After all, they lived off ice cubes, didn't they? She would probably be a welcome and nutritious meal.

The thing's tongue appeared to be lolling as the monster started to trot up the drive. Annie increased her speed, trying to invoke memories of the last time she had needed to run anywhere, a long ago school sports day when she'd come in first by a whisker, giving rise to a fleeting dream of one day entering the Olympics, something later dashed by a teenage obsession with doughnuts. Despite a strict reset operation during her early twenties, it was rare these days that she did more than the occasional hurried stumble after a departing bus.

And then another memory emerged, from that very same school sports day, of being helped onto the back of an animal as it tossed its head and stamped its feet in frustration, culminating in a jerk of its rear which had sent a crying Annie plummeting over the side, landing half in and half out of a school pond positioned unfortunately alongside. A frog had got down her school blazer; a squishy clump of tadpoles into her pocket.

And it had all been the animal's fault.

She had vowed never to enter the presence of something four-legged and bigger than a cat or dog ever again.

And yet here she was.

The creature seemed excited as it lowered its head and

let out a low cry, which, to Annie's horror, was answered from deep in the trees by another, and then another.

Not behind her this time, but in front.

Another monster was moving to cut her off. Annie looked around for somewhere safe—perhaps a hunter's shelter, or even a tree she could climb—but there was nothing but gravel, pine needles, tufts of damp grass, and trees too spindly and branchless to climb.

'Go away!' she shouted, a cry which in deer-speak had to mean 'Welcome! Come here!' because now she could see half a dozen, all sauntering out on to the drive. Their ankles made a strange clicking sound as they trotted in her direction. She looked up as one emerged from the trees right in front of her. She spun around, and something caught on her foot.

She wasn't really sure what had happened except her misplaced footing turned her into a sharp but ungainly pirouette, spinning her in a dizzying circle, the trees and the reindeer a blur. Then she sat down hard on the grass, and looked up through spinning eyes to see an old man in a flat cap leaning over her, a gardening fork in his hands, held across his front, poised to strike.

The madman had sent his beasts to surround her, and now he would close in, end her, and put whatever was left into their feeding trough for a little special treat.

So much for inheriting a manor house.

Annie closed her eyes, slumped back, hoping to bang her head hard enough to pass out.

4

THE GROUNDS KEEPER

THE GRASS, WHILE TOO WET TO BE COMFORTABLE, WAS soft enough. On principle, Annie kept her eyes shut, hoping the world would just disappear, or at the very least, allow her to wake up from a dream/possible nightmare that had begun over a month ago with the arrival of the first, initially distrusted, letter.

'Miss? Are you all reet? Got a bit of muck on your clothes there, just a few droppings and some mud, but we can probably find something up at the house. Sorry about the lassies. Got dinner coming up so they've got their bees in their bonnets. Always get excited by a stranger too. Honestly, sometimes I think I could chuck a ball and half of them would run off to bring it back.'

'I'm dead,' Annie said, staring into the blackness at the back of her eyelids.

The man chuckled. 'Ah, I'm hoping you's not, otherwise I'll have to go and fetch the cart and one of them's wheels is playing up. Canna really leave you lying about for the rats now, can we? The buggers'll get excited. Bad enough to have 'em chewing on me own toes. I think they like the hard bits, so as long as you do that filing thing, you should be all reet.'

Annie's eyes snapped open. 'Rats?'

'Ah, nothing a decent cat wouldn't fix, but her up there, she's got a bit of an allergy. At least, so she says.'

Annie stared at the man. Cherry red cheeks suggested he enjoyed a dram a little too often, but his eyes were bright and his smile kind. Beneath the battered cap, grey hair frizzed out at right angles. Sideburns hung around the corners of a jowly chin like the ends of a scarf he had forgotten to take off.

'Is this the way to Stone Spire Hall?' Annie said, wondering what else she could say. The man was staring not quite at her, but just over her shoulder, as though recalling a series of fond memories. As she spoke, he gave a little shake of the head, his eyes focusing on hers.

'Just round the corner,' he said.

'People keep telling me that. Um … do you live around here?'

'In the cottage.' He stuck a thumb back over his shoulder. 'The one by the gatehouse.'

'What gatehouse? I didn't see any gatehouse.'

'Ah, they moved it. After they drowned the old village for the reservoir.'

'After they—' Annie gave up trying to make sense of things. The man reached out a hand and Annie let him help her sit up. His hand was like a lump of warm, gnarled wood.

'Crossing the fells?' the man said. 'This here's private land, but no one much cares as long as you don't start no fires. If you're heading for Windon Fell, cut through the woods here and follow the new path round the lake. Aren't no signs, but there's only one path, so you won't get much lost.'

Annie shook her head. 'I'm looking for Stone Spire Hall.'

The man chuckled. 'Not many as trying to do that.'

Annie winced. 'You see ... apparently I own it. My name is Annie Collins. It belonged to my grandfather, Wilfred, who died a few weeks ago. I actually didn't know he was still alive, so when I got a letter informing me that I had inherited a country estate, I was just a little bit surprised, not to mention sceptical.'

As soon as Annie had said her name, the man's whole demeanour had changed. His jovial smile was replaced by a look that bordered on reverence. He took a step back and removed his cap, revealing a shiny bald strip between the remnants of his hair. For a moment Annie thought he meant to take a knee, then he turned as one of the reindeer got too close and swiped at it with his cap.

'Mistress,' he said. 'We wondered if you'd come. Me name be Les, but you can just call me Mr. Fairbrother, if it suits you. I'm the estate's caretaker and grounds keeper, like me father was before me, in the service of the Collinses for three generations. It's a pleasure to serve.'

'Ah, thanks. Please put your cap back on, you must be cold.'

'Born out of the woods, will no doubt die in the woods,' Mr. Fairbrother said, somewhat cryptically. 'I do apologise for the fright the lassies caused you. If you'd like me to build an enclosure, give me a holler.'

'They run free? How many do you have?'

Mr. Fairbrother smiled and started counting on his fingers in what Annie could only assume was a local dialect.

'Yan, tyan, tethera, methera, pimp, sethera....' After a few more which left Annie hopelessly lost, he looked up and smiled. 'Couple of dozen. Your grandfather, they were his pleasure.'

'And they don't get lost?'

'Aye, from time to time. Usually come home again when they're hungry. And everyone round here knows where they're from.' He gave a chuckle and smiled off into space. 'There was this one time one got into Bob Slater's garden, chewed through half his cabbages. Guy was spitting fire, but your grandfather, he sent old Bob a couple of bottles from the cellar, and that shut him up.'

'Is that right?'

'Yeah, your grandfather, he was a wonderful man.'

Annie just nodded, not wishing to contradict him with her own opinion of a man she could remember meeting—and even then only briefly—no more than a handful of times, and not at all since her tenth birthday. Twenty-seven years later and she'd all but forgotten that he even existed.

'So … the house? It's near?'

'Just round the corner. I'll show you if you like.'

'Please.'

'All reet. This way then.'

Mr. Fairbrother shouldered his fork and wandered off, checking over his shoulder to see if Annie was following. A few of the reindeer still stood nearby, and as Les moved away they snorted, shook their antlers and began to move closer, as though the order to feed had been given, so Annie hurried to catch up with the old man.

'Don't worry, they's just curious,' Mr. Fairbrother told her, giving a little chuckle. 'Your grandfather, from time to time he'd let 'em in the house, and I think they smell him on you.'

'We'll have to talk about a fence,' Annie said, eyeing the animals wearily, convinced that she was about to discover that her great inheritance was nothing more than a cattle shed in the middle of a field. Trees still hemmed them in on both sides, and the meandering drive refused to give up its secrets. As they crested a low rise, however, up ahead, the trees began to thin, and the lake came back into view.

'Ah, nearly there,' Mr. Fairbrother said, adjusting his cap with one gnarled hand. 'Does seem this old drive is getting longer as me own days get shorter.'

The drive cut back to the right, turning out of sight beyond the tree line. The lakeside came into view, a little wooden jetty extending out into the water, a couple of rowing boats tied up at its end. Just a little way offshore, a small island poked out of the water, topped by a stand of trees. She was still staring at it, trying to make out a bird sitting in the higher branches of one of the trees when Les said, 'Ah, there she is. The old homestead.'

Annie turned, and her breath caught in her throat. 'Oh … my.'

'She's still got the looks, even at her age, hasn't she?'

Annie's knees felt weak, and she reached out for something to support her, finding, in a sudden moment of shock, only the antler of another inquisitive reindeer. As she jumped away, the magical spell cast by seeing the house for the first time was broken. In doing so, however, she was able to appreciate a little better the full extent of what apparently now belonged to her.

Set among trees and overgrown gardens Les was perhaps struggling to manage, Stone Spire Hall was part manor house, part castle. Whoever had built it had struggled to decide on any particular style, with one wing all Elizabethan black and white with overhanging wooden eaves above cast iron window frames, while another was granite stone and raincloud grey, rising four storeys, with even a tower room protruding from one corner, and what looked like a balcony surrounding it, topped with battlements.

'Used to take me own breath away too, Miss, back when I was a lad and coming back from school. Every single time. And if you think this is nice, wait until you see it at Christmas time.'

'It's … magnificent. I can't believe it's mine. This is like a fairytale come true.'

Mr. Fairbrother chuckled. 'Plumbing's a bit shoddy and there's damp in some of the bathrooms.'

'Bathrooms … as in, more than one?'

'There's a fair few kicking about, I suppose. But only three we really use. Others are a bit dusty. Most are in the guest quarters, but old Lord Wilf never had no guests. Bit of a recluse, he was.'

'A bit of a….' Annie could only shake her head. 'I'm still struggling with this. I mean, I'm a bank clerk. I took a week off to come up here, and now I find out my grandfather was a reclusive landowner who owned a mansion and a patch of land—'

'A few hundred acres, more or less, although I don't remember exactly off the top of me old head.'

'—in the Lake District, and I didn't even know?' She flapped her hands. 'This is insane.'

Mr. Fairbrother chuckled. 'Quite, quite.'

'I don't know where to start.'

'Well, she'll sort you out.'

'Who?'

'Mrs. Growell. The housekeeper.'

'Mrs. Growl?'

'That's right. Fearsome as they come, is Mrs. Growell. I mean, it was your grandfather who owned the place, but it was her who ran it. With an iron fist and all.' Les turned and pointed across the open gardens at a small cottage nestled among the trees on the far side. 'That be my humble abode over there. Safest place on the property.' Les chuckled again. 'There was many a winter night when I'd open the door to find your grandfather outside, wanting a place to hide.'

5

THE HOUSE

THE LANE LED THROUGH THE GARDENS TO A WIDER approach that ended in a turning circle in front of the front entrance. Up close, Stone Spire Hall was even more imposing, but signs of neglect were slowly making themselves visible, from cracks in windows taped over to drainpipes coming detached, and she wouldn't have been surprised to find signs of rot in some of the woodwork on the east wing.

'I'll just give her a shout, tell her you're here,' Mr. Fairbrother said, holding up his hands and backing away towards the front door. 'Otherwise she's liable to think you's a trespasser and get her broom out.'

Annie waited, unable to shake her nerves as she stared up at the windows of the imposing manor house. Was this really hers? She was still in a state of disbelief. The place was enormous; there had to be fifty rooms at least, just from looking at the number of windows. The porch alone was bigger than her bedsit, and the ornate flower pots standing by the front door looked more expensive than anything she owned. She'd been forced to live off Cup

Noodles for three days just to scrape enough money together for the train ticket, and now here she was, faced with unbelieveable wealth, belonging to family she hadn't even known existed.

Starting at the top floor, she started counting the windows, just for an estimate. Six, seven, eight—

She let out a little gasp as a face appeared at one in an attic room right above her, then was gone as quickly as it had come. Annie took a step back, trying to see better, but the sun was now glinting off the glass, making it impossible to see anything, and as the seconds passed, she wondered if it was just her mind playing tricks on her.

No, she had definitely seen someone. Perhaps it was the housekeeper, but she'd got the impression that Mrs. Growell was older, and the face she had seen had been young, perhaps even younger than herself.

The front door opened, and Mr. Fairbrother stepped out. He had taken off his cap and now held it clutched across his chest as he puffed out his cheeks, a look of concern on his face. Annie stared at the dark entrance. At first a shadow appeared, morphing into the shape of a tall, imposing woman. She wore all white, and had she worn a hood Annie might have mistaken her for a nun. Instead, as Annie took a step closer, she realised Mrs. Growell's hair was tied up in a net, a bleached white pinafore tied around her waist. On her hands she wore thick oven gloves.

'Um, hello,' Annie said, taking a couple of tentative steps forward. 'I'm Annie Collins.'

Mrs. Growell stared at her. Annie guessed she was in her sixties, her face all angular lines as though she had been made out of origami. It was possible a smile might help, but none looked forthcoming.

'Dinner will be at five p.m. sharp,' Mrs. Growell said. 'Not a minute later. I'll stamp out the ghost of your grandfather's tardiness if it's the last thing I do. Mr. Fairbrother will show you to your rooms.'

With that, she was gone, turning and sweeping back into the house. Annie, more and more convinced this was some weird dream, stood and stared until she realised Mr. Fairbrother was beckoning her forward.

'Come on, lassie, let's get you inside,' he said. 'Evening comes early at this time of the year, and the cold round here comes earlier still.'

Annie still found it hard to move, but she looked down at her feet as though to will them forward, and at last managed to get them moving. She climbed a set of steps to a door that was wide enough for five people to stand side by side, and stopped again. A huge flagstone porch waited inside, beyond which were another set of traditional doors, their frosted glass making it impossible to see through. She wondered where Mrs. Growell had gone, then noticed a small door to the left. A wrought iron sign embedded into the wood conveniently said KITCHENS.

'Should I take off my shoes?' Annie asked Mr. Fairbrother, as she noticed a rack of boots and other outdoor footwear just inside the door.

'Not unless you want cold feet,' Mr. Fairbrother said. 'Are you ready? Not got the fire going yet, but give me half an hour.'

He pushed open the inside doors, and Annie's breath caught in her throat. She found herself staring into a hall out of the pages of a Medieval history book. Towering walls adorned with tapestries, ancient spears and swords, mounted animal heads, and elaborate, ornate candelabras led up to arching wooden eaves adorned with carved animals and forest scenes. At the far end of the room was a massive fireplace piled high with embers. A tall stone chimney stretched up to the ceiling, but out of its upper reaches stretched several large metal pipes, distributing the fire's heat to the upper floors.

Around the fireplace stood several large chairs. Annie took a couple of steps forward, then jumped at the feel of something under her shoes. The pile rug was so thick she could have lost her flat's keys in it.

'This here's the main reception hall,' Mr. Fairbrother said. 'If you ever have a party—not that Lord Wilf ever did, mind—this would be where you serve up all your little sausages on sticks and the like.' He gave a little chuckle. 'Doors to the left go to the banquet hall.'

'There's another one?'

'Just a big table and a few paintings, really. Seats thirty-five comfortable like, but you could get fifty at a push if you went knee to knee.'

'I don't think I know that many people.'

'That'll be all that modern living and all that,' Mr. Fairbrother said. 'Everyone wants to know what everyone's eating for dinner, but don't know why they's eating it, do they?'

'I suppose not.'

'And through that little side door, and down the little corridor, that's the library.'

Annie hadn't even noticed the little door tucked behind a tall display case until Mr. Fairbrother had pointed it out.

'This place is enormous.'

Mr. Fairbrother chuckled again. 'Could get some cracking games of hide'n'seek going on.'

There was a certain hint of nostalgia about the way he spoke, as though pining for bygone days.

'Did my grandfather have a lot of friends?' she asked.

'Nae, none to speak of,' Mr. Fairbrother said. 'Kept himself to himself.' He clapped his hands together. 'Reet, better get you up to your rooms. You just came with that little bag, did you?'

Annie lifted up her rucksack. 'I'm afraid so. I've got an overnight bag in a locker at Quimbeck train station. To be quite honest, I wasn't expecting to find anything except a barn in a field, if that. I'm still waiting for the catch.'

'I can bring in some salmon for tomorrow if you'd like.'

Annie laughed, creating a little echo. It felt weird, but welcome at the same time. 'I didn't mean that kind of catch. Like, when am I going to wake up?'

'Let me know the time you require and I'll have a rooster ready outside your door,' Mr. Fairbrother said, but the smirk on his face told Annie he was getting into the joke. 'Can train them up with accuracy to twenty minutes,' he said. 'Not an exact science, but they's stubborn buggers.'

'This can't be real,' Annie said. 'This can't be mine. I mean, until recently I didn't even know Grandfather was still alive.'

'There's a tale to tell there, I imagine,' Mr. Fairbrother said. 'But that can all wait. We'd better get you up the stairs and sorted out before her down there has a tantrum. Likes her timekeeping, she does, and the Master was a horror for getting her knickers in a twist. Did it on purpose, half the time. Showing up at five oh five and all that. Drove her bonkers. By the way, give us your locker key and I'll go up there later and get your bag.'

'Thank you.'

'Reet, are you ready?'

Annie shouldered her rucksack. 'Lead the way.'

They went through a side door to the right. Mr. Fairbrother pointed out rooms as they passed, from an armoury full of rusting swords and bows to an ornate study, a games room with a full sized snooker table standing in the centre, and even a gallery, lined with dusty oil paintings of Lake District country scenes.

There appeared to be multiple staircases, from wide, sweeping ones to narrow, spiraling types that vanished like corkscrews into the ceiling. Mr. Fairbrother led her up one —'Because you're less likely to bump into her up here'— to the third floor, along a wide, carpeted corridor to a set of double doors about halfway along.

'This was the Master's suite,' Mr. Fairbrother said. 'Have a look. If it's a bit overwhelming for you, we've got plenty of other rooms. Give me half an hour's notice and I'll have one made up.'

He turned and started back up the corridor.

'Wait.'

'Aye, Mistress?'

'Ah … how do I contact you?'

Les smiled. 'Reet. Got a string next to the bed. Give it a tug and I'll be up in five minutes, unless I'm out in the grounds, in which case she'll give me a holler. Got a little bell, see. Not quite all this phones and modern technology and all that, but it works if I'm paying attention.'

He started walking away once more, but again Annie called him back.

'Aye, Mistress?'

'Ah, Mr. … ah, Fairbrother … thank you for everything.'

Mr. Fairbrother smiled. He pulled his hat off his head, gave it a tug, then put it back on again.

'All in a day's work, Mistress. I must say, it's nice having someone around to serve again. We—even her down there —were worried you wouldn't come. What would we have done then? Bunch of headless chickens, the whole lot of us.'

He gave a little bow, then headed off. This time Annie said nothing, just let him go. Then, when he was out of sight, she turned to the doors, took a deep breath, and prepared to push through into a world she had never known.

6

LOCKED OUT

SHE TRIED THE HANDLE, BUT THE DOORS DIDN'T MOVE. Annie suppressed a sigh.

Locked.

She looked around at the empty corridor, nerves jumping. Was this where the reality kicked in, the cameramen came out of some hidden door, and a TV presenter with slicked hair and an Instagram smile jumped in front of her with a microphone?

How did you like it, Miss Collins? How did it feel, just for a few minutes, to think you were a Lady of the Manor?

But nothing happened. The corridor stayed empty. She shook the door again, and it still didn't budge.

Locked. Just locked.

She headed off after Les, but when she got to the end of the corridor, she found a door standing where the stairs had once been. Frowning, she gave it a tug, but this one also seemed to be locked.

She wondered how she hadn't noticed it. Then, giving it a thorough inspection, she realised that it slid on a runner, and being the same design as the surrounding walls, it had hitherto stood unnoticed. Annie gave it a tug, but like her suite door, it was definitely locked.

Beside it, however, another staircase led up, this one a narrow spiral barely wide enough for one person, let alone for two to pass. Annie crept up, one step at a time, feeling a strange sense of intrusion. She was the trespasser in her own home, like a naughty school kid sneaking into the teachers-only areas.

The staircase ended at a narrow landing with a bright red carpet. Wallpaper in an autumn floral pattern needed replacing. A light switch on the wall didn't switch on the light, the bulb of which was covered in a layer of dust. The light, however, was coming through a door that led outside. Another closed door led into a room to Annie's left, but it was also locked. Making a mental note to ask Mr. Fairbrother for some kind of master key, she decided to go outside. The house, while beautiful and vast, was a little stuffy, as though it would really benefit from a few open windows.

The door led out to a stone balcony edged with actual battlements. Annie gasped at the view as the wind ruffled her hair. The carpet of forest turned into rolling fells stretching away into the distance, with the glittering lake in the middle. In the distance, some of the Lake District's tallest fells had a dusting of early season snow.

With one hand on the stone battlements to keep her steady against the buffeting wind, Annie followed the balcony as it circled the tower room, taking in a complete panorama of the surrounds. Behind, to the house's north, the forest was thicker, but about a mile distant the roofs of a cluster of houses appeared among the trees. She was a long way from Quimbeck, the last recognisable settlement of any size she had seen on her way here, but the buildings suggested some kind of village.

A few spots of rain had appeared in the air. Annie finished her circuit and had just reached the door when a flurry of colour appeared against the small wrought-iron framed window in the door's centre.

Annie wasn't quick enough to see what it was, but when she tried the handle she found the door now locked.

'Hey!' she shouted, and gave the handle a frantic tug, but the door wouldn't budge. She stared at the iron door handle in dismay, then, with a rising sense of panic welling up inside her, she went back to the battlements and leaned over.

'Help!' she shouted. 'I'm locked out.'

The rain was getting heavier. With no way to shelter, Annie had no choice but to continue hollering into the rising wind.

The garden was deserted, though, and for as far as she could see there wasn't anyone around. The clouds were looming, and in the distance a bolt of lightning crashed into a hilltop.

'Help me!' Annie shouted again. 'Someone? Anyone? Help! I'm locked out!'

Something was moving in the trees just beyond the edge of the gardens. Annie waved her arms over her head, thinking it might be Mr. Fairbrother, but as the shape emerged out on to the path, her heart sank.

One of the reindeer, its face turned up to look at her. While she couldn't see its expression over the distance, she was certain it was mocking her, enjoying a little payback for her earlier dislike.

'I'm sorry!' she shouted. 'I didn't mean it! I just don't like anything that reminds me of a horse because I fell off one once! Please ... go and fetch Mr. Fairbrother, or something.'

Another reindeer appeared out of the trees, then

another. Within a couple of minutes, there were more than twenty of them, all standing in a group, faces looking up at her. Annie was now getting soaked, and she was certain the creatures were enjoying it.

'I love a good steak!' she shouted, even though it had been years since she'd been able to afford anything but the cheapest cuts of meat. 'And I fancy a new rug. Or several!'

The reindeer continued to stare at her. Another lightning bolt flashed, this one a little closer, making Annie flinch, but the animals on the ground seemed unconcerned.

'I'm not going to jump!' she shouted. 'You're not going to get the satisfaction!'

Although, as she thought about it, she wondered if there was a drainpipe or perhaps a sliding roof nearby, in case she got really desperate. After taking a look over the battlements and finding only a sheer drop, she grimaced and shook her head.

Nope.

She was just cursing herself for leaving her bag containing her phone outside her grandfather's old rooms when a figure came running out of the house below. Weaving through the flowerbeds towards the reindeer, it carried a cane in one hand and a length of rope in the other.

'Mr. Fairbrother!' Annie screamed, as the figure began herding the deer away from the flowerbeds and back towards the trees. 'Mr.—'

He stopped and looked up, following the reindeers' gaze. At first Annie didn't think he had seen her, then he pulled off his cap, gave it a squeeze, then patted the nearest reindeer on the neck.

'Enjoying the view up there? Got an umbrella in the kitchen if need be. I'd be careful of the storm, though. Got a conductor up there, right above your head, but he might be on the blink.'

'Someone's locked me out!'

She couldn't hear his response over a rumble of thunder, but he gave her a wave that could mean anything, then hurried back to the house. He disappeared out of sight just as the rain picked up, drenching Annie with great freezing drops that struck as hard as the arrows of an invading enemy.

Ten minutes later, she was sitting by the fire in the main hall, a thick, musty smelling blanket around her shoulders, while Mr. Fairbrother stood to one side, cowering somewhat under the glare of Mrs. Growell, who stood on the other, arms folded, her face pinched into a scowl.

'You must make sure the Mistress has a key,' she snapped at Mr. Fairbrother. 'What with the old locks on this place, and the wind….'

Mr. Fairbrother, for his part, gave a sheepish grimace. 'I'm not sure you could go blaming the locks,' he said. 'After all, they don't go locking themselves, do they?'

Mrs. Growell glared at him, and something unspoken passed between them. Annie, who was still struggling to keep a grounding in reality, didn't feel it her place to comment. Instead, she waved a hand and gave them her best disarming smile.

'It was probably just the wind. Nothing to worry about.'

'Yes, the wind,' Mrs. Growell said.

'The wind, my cobblers,' Mr. Fairbrother muttered under his breath, but Mrs. Growell didn't appear to hear.

'Mistress, I'd suggest you stick to your rooms and the

common areas for the time being,' Mrs. Growell said. 'This old place has a number of quirks that can feel a little … unwelcoming to a stranger.'

Annie put up a hand. 'Um, can I just make a request? It's really okay not to call me Mistress. I mean, it feels a little strange. I didn't even know my grandfather was still alive until I started getting these letters, and then of course I found out that he wasn't, but you know, I thought he died years ago. My mother never said a word.'

Mrs. Growell and Mr. Fairbrother exchanged a glance as though Annie were speaking a foreign language.

'And … and … until yesterday I was wondering how on earth I was going to pay my electricity bill. I mean, my fridge was broken, but I unplugged it sometimes anyway, just to keep the bills down. I had to empty the coins bottle I save for bus tickets in order to afford the train, and I get here and it's like a manor house surrounded by gardens and forests with reindeer running about, and there are battlements, and there even seems to be some kind of ghost—'

Mrs. Growell huffed, then shook her head at Mr. Fairbrother.

'The Mistress looks hungry,' she said. 'How inconsiderate of me to not prepare a welcome snack.'

'You knew I was coming?'

Mrs. Growell's nostrils flared. 'Does the place not look recently cleaned?'

'Well, yes, but my standards are not high. My hoover broke last month and I've been using these sticky pad things I got out of Poundstretcher while I save up for a new one.'

'How inconvenient.'

'I mean, they picked up all the hairs and crumbs and stuff, but it's not exactly a deep clean—'

Mrs. Growell nodded. 'You can't beat a SEBO Pro Boost, but they don't come cheap. Just ask the Royal Family.' She gave a little shudder, then clapped her hands together. 'So. Mr. Fairbrother, do you know what happened to the key to the Master's suite?'

'I could hazard a guess—'

'In its absence please arrange a guest suite for the Mistress while we find a spare. You have forty minutes until dinner. Ensure that the Mistress is prompt. I abhor tardiness.'

With that, Mrs. Growell turned and marched out of the room. As soon as the door to the kitchens closed behind her, Mr. Fairbrother grinned at Annie, then gave a mock salute.

'Aye, sir.'

7

DINNER AND AFTER

'I SUPPOSE THIS'LL HAVE TO DO TO TIDE YOU OVER A FEW days,' Mr. Fairbrother said, standing by the open door, which he gave an affectionate pat. 'At least he opens.'

'Do you think you'll be able to find the key to Grandfather's suite tomorrow?'

'Will do me damnedest,' Mr. Fairbrother said. 'In the meantime, you have a nice night, and I'll see you on the morrow. I'm up and about seven o'clock sharp.' Then, leaning forward a little as though afraid of being overheard, he added, 'I'd suggest you lock your door on the inside while you're asleep. Not that there's owt to worry about, but you know, place as big as this, lights not working all that well, 'tis easy to try the wrong doors from time to time. Best to be safe, eh.'

Annie gave a nervous nod, then said goodbye to Mr. Fairbrother.

Inside, the room and connecting bathroom were a little bigger than a hotel suite, but the décor was definitely on the more extravagant side. A floral bedspread matched the curtains, while the carpet was rose-red. A pot of dried flowers sat on a pretty dressing table while framed paintings of more flowers adorned the walls. Everything had a faint smell of lavender. When she checked the bedding, however, Annie was surprised to find it freshly laundered. Mr. Fairbrother had sat with her during dinner —a delicious bowl of minestrone followed by a large slice of beef pie and then a homemade fudge pudding for dessert—while Mrs. Growell had regularly marched to and from the kitchens to deliver more courses. She had seen no other people, so either they kept rooms made up just in case people appeared out of nowhere, or there was someone else here.

The face at the window.

Annie hadn't found a good time to ask with Mr. Fairbrother keeping up a monologue about changes in the weather, trials and tribulations with the reindeer, how a hiker had dropped a sandwich wrapper down by the lake, and a dozen other small qualms and issues, while he stared mostly into the fire, as though unaware Annie was even there. And apart from thanking Mrs. Growell for each course, Annie hadn't been able to question the housekeeper, either.

Still, now that night had fallen and she had established a place she could sleep in this massive, rambling old house, she figured it was best to find out what was going on sooner rather than later. She found a glass in a cupboard below the sink in the bathroom, filled it with water that initially spat and spurted from the faucet as though it hadn't been used in some time, then sat down on her bed and pulled out her phone.

Two bars of signal. It would have to do.

She checked the time in Canada then dialed her mother's number.

'Hello?'

A man's voice, not her mother's, and so faint and scratchy it was hard to hear. Glancing at her phone display, Annie saw that the signal mast icon was flashing on and off.

'Ah, hi, is that Jack? It's Annie.'

'Annie … ah, Annie! How are you, dear?'

'Um, fine. Is Mum there?'

'She's gone away with a friend. Polar bear viewing, or something. Can I have her call you back?'

Jack's voice was so faint Annie could barely catch his words. 'No, it's okay. I'll try her on her mobile in the morning.'

'Sure thing. See you.'

Jack hung off without fuss, leaving Annie staring at the phone in her hand. There wouldn't be any point trying her mother's mobile; her mother tended to go off the grid, and wouldn't have reception even if she did remember to turn it on. Annie let out a sigh, then got up and walked to the window. Three bars. Satisfied, she dialed Julie's number.

'So, how is it?'

Annie smiled. 'It exists. My god, the place is monstrous.'

'Squee! I knew it. Oh, wow. How does it feel to be the Lady of the Manor? Oh goodness, how exciting!'

'It's totally weird, and I'm not sure what to make of it, to be honest. It doesn't feel real, and I keep expecting to find out they've made a mistake. But there's definitely a big old house, complete with crazy live-in staff—'

She broke off, her arm going limp, the phone almost slipping out of her fingers.

'Annie? What is it? You were saying?'

But Annie was staring at the door, where the handle was rattling at intervals of a couple of seconds: rattle, quiet, rattle.

'I think someone's trying to get in.'

'Oh my. Is it one of the staff?'

'I have no idea.'

'Is there a gardener? Did he look like George Clooney?'

Annie continued to stare at the door. 'He might have done once. About seventy-five years ago. I think it's someone else.'

'Oh my. Keep me on the line in case they try to murder you. Do you want me to call the police on Darren's phone?'

Annie, her fingertips tingling with nerves, crept away from the window and slowly approached the door as the handle continued to rattle.

'Is there a peephole?' Julie whispered on the phone Annie had pressed to her ear.

'Unfortunately not,' Annie said, reaching down, stretching her fingers around the rattling door handle.

Three, two, one ... she silently counted down, then grabbed hold of the door knob. For a moment she felt resistance on the other side, then she gave it a sharp rattle of her own.

'Pack it in!' she snapped, as a surprised gasp came from the other side of the door, followed by the patter of feet as someone ran away up the hall. Intending to chase down the potential intruder, Annie grabbed the door handle and twisted it sharply.

Instead of the door swinging inward, however, the door knob popped out of its fitting and came away in her hand.

'What's going on?' Julie hissed.

Annie stared at the door knob.

'Small problem,' she said.

8

A GHOST IN THE HALLS

IN THE END, ANNIE WAS ABLE TO GET THE DOOR OPEN BY sliding the knob back into the fitting and holding the door still while she turned it. Julie had needed to get her children ready for bed but had demanded an update later, leaving Annie alone as she carefully opened the door and peered out into the corridor.

Empty, as Annie had expected, but to her surprise she found a bottle of polish and a duster lying on the carpet outside the door. The knob on the outside was freshly gleaming, although why anyone had felt the need to polish the door knobs at this time of night, Annie couldn't understand. As she took a few steps up the corridor to the adjacent room, she saw the door knob there looked dull and dusty, so either the mysterious cleaner hadn't got to it yet, or hers had been singled out for special treatment.

But who could the mysterious cleaner be?

The gasp and patter of feet had certainly not belonged to either Mrs. Growell or Mr. Fairbrother, but the very presence of the polish and the rag suggested this was no ghost, unless it was a very real one with a penchant for cleaning. Frowning, Annie shook her head.

Making sure to lock her own door then pocket the key, Annie set off in pursuit of the mysterious cleaner.

The footsteps had seemed to head left, but within a few steps Annie came to staircases leading both up and down, so realised she was going to have to settle for a general exploration instead. Avoiding going into any room where she might get locked in, she settled for trying door knobs and peering into any unlocked rooms to see what was inside.

The other rooms on her floor were bedrooms rather like hers, although most had plastic covers over the bedclothes or were not made up at all, as though they were rarely used. Up a flight of stairs she passed her grandfather's suite—still locked—and this time she avoided the stairs to the tower room and the balcony where she had been locked outside.

Creeping downstairs, she passed a gallery filled with paintings, its lights off, and then peered through a window into the armoury, lines of rusty swords and spears in glass cases like the bones of some long lost army. Past the banquet hall on the bottom floor she found a couple of large, empty rooms which would likely make good places for wedding ceremonies, especially one which had a terrace out to the house's side with views of the forest and the lake. Now, though, everything was dark, not a single light penetrating the darkness.

Annie quickly realised that she would never find the mysterious cleaner if she didn't want to be found, because the house didn't follow any regular layout. Narrow corridors disappeared between rooms, leading to tiny winding staircases that seemed designed purely to confuse people. Annie, feeling a childish sense of wonder as she remembered something Mr. Fairbrother had said, couldn't help but imagine the epic games of hide'n'seek that small children could have. She came across more than one sliding door concealing some hidden chamber or staircase, even a couple of trapdoors, that until she had her bearings better, she didn't dare go down.

Coming to a door that led outside to a gloomy maze of flowerbeds, Annie stepped outside for a moment—keeping one hand on the door handle, just in case—and found herself marvelling at the coolness of the air, the stillness of the dark forest, the calm and peace of the countryside. Expecting to see stars, she peered up at the night sky, but to her surprise it was a dark, invisible blanket. Then, caught in the dim glow of an outside light, something small floated down in front of her.

A snowflake.

It was only November. Annie couldn't imagine what winter might be like if it was snowing already.

She had a sudden vision of the house lit up with Christmas lights, shining like a beacon in the dark. Her parents had always kept Christmas to a minimum— decorations in the living room only, and even then, only in the corner with the tree and over their ornamental fireplace—and Annie had always felt jealous of her school friends whose houses were decked out with lights. She had thought about suggesting something to Troy, but the cracks in their marriage had begun to appear not long after it had begun, and the couple of Christmases they had enjoyed had been overseas ones in the unseasonal climates of Florida and Malaga.

She let out a sigh and turned back to the house.

A blur of movement caught her eye as someone further up the corridor ducked out of sight. This time Annie had got a better view of the person. A girl—blonde-haired, thin, waiflike, dressed in a black and white dress—had slipped down a side corridor that Annie remembered led to a narrow back staircase. Shutting the door quickly, Annie ran down the corridor and up a wider staircase leading to the floor above.

Able to move quicker, she made it to the landing and came around the corner just as the girl should have reached the top of the stairs. Annie ducked into an alcove, squeezing in beside a statue of a horse on a stone dais.

A floorboard creaked, just out of sight. Annie held her breath. A shadow fell over the carpet right in front of her, thin, elongated. Annie peered out from behind the statue.

A girl stood in front of her, her back turned, leaning on the corner and peering back towards the staircase she had just ascended as though waiting for Annie to follow. Annie had a chance to study her and marvelled at the girl's attire. She was the most elaborately dressed maid Annie had ever seen. Her dress was a black and white cartoonish array of frills and ribbons, while hair that was almost white but with dyed strands of brown and black was tied into pigtails that trailed over her shoulders, and topped with a little bonnet with just a hint of pink to give her some colour.

Annie took a deep breath. 'I think I caught you,' she said.

The girl let out a wail that was part terror, part excitement. She spun around, nearly falling over, and stared at Annie with eyes and mouth open wide, hands cupped over her cheeks.

She looked so shocked that Annie couldn't help but laugh.

'I didn't mean to startle you,' she said. 'Are you the ghost that's been following me around?'

The girl's expression changed. Still cupping her face

with her hands, she gave a wide smile, as though Annie's estimation made her happy, then gave a childlike giggle.

'I'm Annie,' Annie said. 'Apparently this is now my house. And you are?'

The girl continued to stare at her. Then, breathing one sudden, quick word that Annie wasn't sure had been a word at all, she turned and fled, her feet pattering on the stairs before Annie had even reached the corner of the corridor.

She was left with a bemused grin on her face, and the bones of the word she thought the girl had said.

'Isabella.'

9

BREAKFAST

To Annie's absolute delight, she opened the curtains the next morning to discover the world outside had turned white. A dusting of snow covered everything, from the flowerbeds to the tops of the trees. The distant fells were domes of white, and even the lake had silvery patches of ice.

The shower in her en suite bathroom was a bit cranky, and for a while Annie didn't think she'd get any hot water, but eventually a little trickled out, and after drying and getting dressed she headed downstairs feeling refreshed after a long and dreamless night's sleep.

Through a window near the main entrance she saw Mr. Fairbrother using a plastic shovel to clear snow off the path from the car park up to the door, a Christmas hat modified with ear muffs stretched over his head. A small upper window had been left open to allow in some fresh air, and the sound of a jovial whistle drifted inside.

Annie watched him for a while, wondering whether she ought to offer to help. When she turned, however, she found Mrs. Growell standing nearby, hands crossed over her stomach. Impeccably dressed in her kitchen uniform, the woman looked like a vampire dressing down for a costume ball. Recovering her shock at finding the woman so close, Annie muttered a brief 'Good morning,' and offered a smile.

'Good morning, Mistress,' Mrs. Growell said, not sounding particularly happy about it but forcing a hint of a smile. 'Are you ready for breakfast?'

'Uh … thank you.'

'A table has been prepared.'

Mrs. Growell turned and went through the propped-open door into the reception hall, where a table had been set up in front of the fire gently flickering in the grate. Annie followed like a child on her first day at boarding school, and sat down where Mrs. Growell indicated.

'Coffee or tea, Mistress? Or would you prefer juice? We have orange, grapefruit, or elderberry.'

'Uh … coffee.'

'Excellent. Before your meal? Or after? Your grandfather always took it before.'

'Um, that's great.'

Annie sat awkwardly as Mrs. Growell reeled off a list of possible breakfast options, eventually agreeing to a bowl of cornflakes and a bacon sandwich. A few minutes later, Mrs. Growell returned with a waiter's trolley, and unloaded Annie's order onto the table, along with a bowl of sliced fruit.

'If your grandfather had eaten a little better, we might have got a couple more years out of him,' she said, a note of sadness in her voice. Then, recovering her composure, she added, 'Enjoy your breakfast, Mistress. If there's anything else you require, please ring the bell.'

'Um, thanks.'

Mrs. Growell turned and headed for the entrance to

the kitchens. At the top of the stairs leading down, she stopped and turned back, pausing to watch Annie for a few seconds. Feeling a little awkward, Annie grinned and gave her a little wave. Mrs. Growell simply nodded, then descended the stairs into the basement servant quarters.

'Too weird,' Annie muttered. Her brain didn't feel like eating, but her stomach disagreed, so a few minutes of thoughtful reflection later, she found the food had all gone. Everything, she realised, in retrospect, had been perfect. The bacon was perfectly grilled, the bread perfectly toasted, even the cornflakes soaked just long enough in the milk to be damp but retaining their crunch.

Annie reached for the bell to call Mrs. Growell to take away her plates, then paused. Despite the reality of the situation, this wasn't a hotel, and it felt weird having people waiting on her. She got up, stacked her empty plates and carried them to the stairs.

In her hunt for the mysterious Isabella, Annie had seen much of the house and its vast array of rooms and corridors, but she was yet to go down the stairs into the basement servants' quarters. She felt a little like an intruder as she descended an underlit staircase to a corridor at the bottom.

She was underground now, she remembered. The air felt a little muggy, and the corridor was poorly lit. Doors led off on either side, closed, unmarked. Mr. Fairbrother claimed to live in a cottage near the lake, but perhaps Mrs. Growell lived down here, maybe even Isabella, assuming she wasn't just a very real ghost.

At the end of the corridor was a large pair of double doors with KITCHENS written on one side and STAFF ONLY on the other. Annie, pretending she couldn't read, backed up against one door and pushed her way through.

'Uh … what on earth?'

The kitchen—higher ceilinged than it ought to have been, suggesting it rose into some kind of atrium at the side of the house—was a kitchen in name only. It clearly had cookers and stoves and cupboards like any other kitchen, but otherwise it appeared like the internal workings of a Christmas-themed candy factory, all bright reds and greens and golds. Pipes and pistons stuck out from everywhere, bubbles rose through clear tubes and little toy figures walked along conveyors, falling into chutes which would cause whistles to sound, followed by a rush of air and the figures appearing again out of a little door somewhere else to start the revolving process all over.

Annie clapped her hands together as she burst into laughter.

'How wonderful!'

A door opened at the end, and Mrs. Growell entered, carrying a large bag of flour in her arms. At the sight of Annie she let out a gasp and dropped the bag.

For a moment everything seemed to go still, a single second lasting for a lifetime as the bag of flour descended through the air.

Then it struck beautiful ornate and colourful tiles, and exploded into a white cloud.

'Oh, I'm so sorry!'

'What are you doing in my kitchen? Get out! I knew you'd be trouble from the moment I laid eyes on you. Get *out!*'

Annie started to back away towards the door. Mrs. Growell stepped forward out of the plume of flour made worse by air filters in the walls on either side which only served to spread it around. Her face, spotted with flour, looked like a thundercloud as she reached up and pulled a cord on the wall.

A muffled bell sounded somewhere upstairs. Annie

backed up and found herself against the doors just as one opened, knocking into her. She stepped forward, slipped, and her plates fell out of her arms.

That same crazy timeless second repeated itself. Annie had just a moment to envisage the crockery shattering all over the floor, then to her amazement, her coffee cup landed face up on a pile of flour, her plate struck Mrs. Growell's shoe and rolled sideways, and her cereal bowl hit Mrs. Growell in the stomach, only for the woman to stick out a deft hand and catch it, a dribble of unfinished milk trickling down her wrist. Only a fork hit the tiles, where it made a tinkling jump and lay still.

'Oh, sorry, dear, was just on my way in,' Mr. Fairbrother said. 'Did you—oh, blimey.' He chuckled. 'Been snowing in here, too?'

Mrs. Growell's eyes flared, and had they burst into flames, Annie wouldn't have been surprised.

'You have the bell,' she said, almost too quietly to be heard over the sound of the mechanisation. 'You need assistance, you ring the bell. If you have a question, you ring the bell. If the house is on fire … you ring the bell.'

'I ring the bell,' Annie said. 'Got it.'

'*Out!*'

Annie didn't wait to be ordered again, backing through the door, running back along the service corridor and up the stairs to the main entrance before Mrs. Growell could shoot lasers at her or set loose some hounds of hell on her trail. She slipped on a pair of boots and stepped outside, only then allowing herself to take a long, slow breath of cool, winter air.

She would apologise to the housekeeper, perhaps when Mrs. Growell's internal volcano had stopped erupting. She seemed to have made an enemy of the woman, but perhaps she had done that already simply by coming here.

As her own thundering heart slowed, and the pretty winter scene began to calm her, Annie wondered about the kitchen. It was like something out of a fairy tale, a room out of a theme park relocated to the middle of nowhere. And with all those weird contraptions rattling away, it was no wonder Mrs. Growell seemed on edge. Being in there all day long would drive anyone mad.

'Sorry about that commotion, Mistress,' came a voice from behind her, and Annie turned to find Mr. Fairbrother standing behind her. Flour flecked his shirt but otherwise he looked the same as he had done yesterday.

'I'm sorry too,' Annie said. 'I shouldn't have gone in there. Next time I'll just ring the bell.'

'Ah, don't worry about that,' Mr. Fairbrother said. 'She's spikey at the best of times. Nothing a hoover didn't sort in a minute or two. Might be an idea to take you over to the village for a bit, though, let her clear her head.'

'The village?'

'Just through the forest there.'

'Oh, I thought I saw some houses through the trees there. Is it big?'

'Handful of houses.'

'Oh, it would be nice to meet a few locals.'

'They'll be looking forward to seeing you too,' Mr. Fairbrother said. 'Been wondering what was going to happen after your grandfather passed.'

'Why's that? What does my grandfather have to do with the village?'

Mr. Fairbrother chuckled. 'A whole lot. You see, he owned it. Which means that now, it belongs to you.'

10

UNDERCASTLE

'Do we have to walk through that forest? Can't we go by car?'

'Ah, track's a little uncertain after a fall,' Mr. Fairbrother said. 'Got a few holes I need to fill in. Be a hassle if we get stuck.'

'But what about the reindeer?'

Mr. Fairbrother chuckled. 'Fed the lassies this morning. Plus, I don't think they're into human flesh as a food source. They was just a little curious yesterday, 'twas all.'

Annie shivered, not just from the cold. The forest track leading away from the back of the house was even narrower than the one she'd taken from the main road, the trees looming over it on both sides. That snow had managed to cover it seemed surprising until a solid gust of wind nearly blew her off her feet.

Mr. Fairbrother chuckled again. 'Well, that was a strong 'un. Almost ended up face down.'

'Is it likely to get worse? I mean, it's only November.'

'Oh, for sure. Snow comes piling in. But there's Christmas, isn't there?'

'Is there?'

Mr. Fairbrother frowned as he turned to her. 'Didn't know your grandfather much at all, did you?'

Annie sighed. 'No, I really didn't.'

'Was quite the character. Nuts, for sure, some would say.' He gave another little chuckle, but this one was more nostalgic, and when Annie looked at him, she noticed a little twinkle in his eye. 'Visionary, would say others.'

'Maybe I'll find out a little more once I can get into his suite,' Annie said.

As if breaking out of a trance, Mr. Fairbrother gave a little shake. 'Aye, aye, we'll hunt out that spare key.' Then, before Annie could ask anything else, he headed down the steps onto the path and marched off in the direction of the forest, leaving Annie hurrying to keep up.

'So, this village,' she said, when she managed to get close enough to be heard without shouting, 'Can you tell me a little more about it?'

'Undercastle,' Mr. Fairbrother said. 'Bit of an in-joke, that. I know old Stone Spire is more of a manor, but I think Lord Wilf had plans to dig a moat or have a portcullis installed, and all that.'

'Is it new or old, or—?'

'A bit of both. You see, 'twas your great-great grandfather who built this place, but in those days, the village was back there, where you see that lake. Water's risen a little since then, due to a dam further down the valley.'

'A dam?'

'Just a small one, like. A bit of hydro. All that modern energy and things. What happened to burning a bit of peat?'

'Ah ... Pete? Oh, *peat.*'

'Anyways, village was likely to end up underwater, but

that was when your grandfather stepped in. Decided to buy up all the vacated homes and move them back a bit.'

'Literally move them?'

'Uh-huh. Brick by brick. I imagine the post-it notes were worse than any snowstorm when they pulled the buggers back off.' Mr. Fairbrother broke into a series of coughing chuckles that took a few steps to overcome.

'That must have taken some effort.'

'For sure. Got everyone involved, he did, lugging those houses back from the shore. Plonked them down on a patch of land and got to landscaping. Wouldn't know the difference now.'

They had made it into the forest now, but rather than the cold gloominess that Annie had anticipated, with the snow hanging from the branches and a dusting on the gravel road it made her feel calm, peaceful.

'So ... this is still a shock to me, and I'm expecting to wake up at any moment, perhaps with a bucket of water thrown over my head, but this village belongs entirely to me?'

Mr. Fairbrother nodded. 'Belongs to the estate.'

'And ... what do the people do? Just, like, live there?'

'Cottage industry,' Mr. Fairbrother said. 'Not sure how your grandfather made his coin?'

'I have no clue. Like I say, as far as I knew, he died years ago.'

'Well, you'll see in a bit.'

They lapsed into silence as they came out of the trees, the village appearing in a little hollow in front of them. Annie couldn't help but shake her head at the sight of it. Picture postcard perfect, the collection of stone-walled cottages tucked along a couple of narrow streets looked straight off a computer screen's background wallpaper, the kind of place everyone dreamed about visiting, but in reality didn't exist. Pretty stone walls bordered gardens with ponds and fountains and fishing gnomes. Slanting roofs hung over latticed windows. Smoke puffed out of chimneys and warm lights glowed behind lace curtains. From somewhere came the gentle tinkle of piano music. There appeared to be no cars, but through a gap in the houses to the right, Annie caught sight of a little steam train sitting in a station, smoke puffing out of its funnel.

'Um … there's a train? The solicitor didn't tell me there was a train.'

'Ah, doesn't run no more. Line got cancelled. They just keep it here for show.'

'But there's smoke coming out of it.'

Mr. Fairbrother shrugged. 'Got to turn the engine over, otherwise she'll rust.'

Annie was still in a state of disbelief. While the village clearly existed, and was so quaint she could have put it on a plate and eaten it with a bowl of ice-cream, there was something missing.

'Where are all the people?' she asked.

Mr. Fairbrother frowned. 'What, it's Monday, hey? Be at work, won't they?'

'Work?'

'Everyone's gotta work. Even your grandfather, although he always said it was more play than work.'

'What exactly did he do to be wealthy enough to own an entire village?'

Mr. Fairbrother chuckled again. 'We'll get that key and you'll see for yourself. Always better to discover than be told, that was one of his sayings.'

They walked into the village, the gravel replaced by cobblestones. They passed a fudge shop and a café with a sign outside advertising local food, a small pub that appeared closed, a greengrocers. A man was standing outside, arranging carrots in a box.

'Reg!' Mr. Fairbrother shouted, making the man jump, almost knocking over the box. 'Come and have a gander at the lassie here.'

Reg turned around. He was a ruddy-faced man in his fifties, hair curled like wool trying to escape a cap pressed tightly over his head. A potbelly suggested he enjoyed a little too much of the fudge up the street, but he had a cheerful, friendly look about him.

'Who's this?' Reg asked. 'Don't tell me we've finally got a tourist.'

'Lord Wilf's daughter,' Mr. Fairbrother said. 'Lass finally showed up.'

'Granddaughter,' Annie corrected.

Reg took off his cap and gave a short bow. Hair exploded out like a sheep making a break for freedom, only to be recaptured when Reg replaced his hat.

'A pleasure,' he said. 'We've been expecting you ever since the old man passed.'

'Ah, thanks.'

Reg gestured at the vegetables and fruit arranged in the boxes. 'Anything you want, it's on the house,' he said.

'Thanks very much.'

'Although, technically it's already yours.'

Annie gave a bashful smile. 'I'm not—'

'Lass is still coming to terms with it all,' Mr. Fairbrother said. 'Sounds like the old man weren't joking about keeping it all under the blankets, so to speak. Own family didn't know what he had going on up here.'

'You shown her the—'

Mr. Fairbrother gave a sharp shake of the head. 'Only just shown up, hasn't she? One step at a time.'

'Shown me the what?'

63

The two old men shared a chuckle. 'The old fire-breather suggested we break her in slowly, so she doesn't go running, or worse, puts the place up for sale,' Mr. Fairbrother said, seemingly ignoring Annie.

'Don't want to go crossing her.'

'Quite.'

Annie put up a hand. 'Ah … I'm right here.'

Reg grinned and turned to her. 'Mistress, we're delighted to welcome you. Perhaps if you have time, you could come down to The Old Goat one evening and give us a proper introduction. I mean, not like we're glad old Wilf is gone or anything….'

'The old goat?'

'Lad means the pub,' Mr. Fairbrother said. 'The Old Goat and Whistle. Just round the corner up yonder.'

'Or pop into Diane's Pancake House or Frank's Fudge. Crying out for something to do. Or perhaps get Tommy to take you out on the boat, up to the gorge.'

Annie held up a hand and smiled. 'I haven't even unpacked my suitcase yet.'

'Lost the old man's room key,' Mr. Fairbrother said. 'I think *she* might have been playing one of her tricks.'

'Wanna get her a proper job,' Reg said, leaning close to Mr. Fairbrother and lowering his voice. Then, looking at Annie, he said, 'Right, better get back to it. These carrots won't stack themselves.'

Annie's ears burned from the information overload as she trailed Mr. Fairbrother down the street. The old man was muttering to himself something about putting in an order of carrots for the reindeer when Annie put a hand on his arm.

'Look,' she said. 'Is there any chance you could tell me what's going on around here? I mean, this village is absolutely lovely, like something out of a guidebook, but there's barely a soul here, there doesn't seem to be a way in or out, and there's even a railway station without a railway line. What kind of a tourist village doesn't have any tourists?'

A shop had come up on their left. Warm light glowed through the windows, and an ornate sign over the door announced Diane's Pancake House.

'Might be time for a pit stop,' Mr. Fairbrother said. 'Plus, Miss Jenkins has a better way with words than me.'

They went in through the door, a little bell tinkling overhead. Inside, the shop smelled of cooking pancakes and chocolate. A few tables were arranged near the windows, but there were no customers. Above a countertop was a mouthwatering menu of pancakes and their fillings.

'Hello there,' came a voice from a backroom, and an elderly woman appeared, folding up a newspaper as she emerged through a hanging curtain showing a picture of a pretty valley in the middle of autumn. The woman was in her late sixties at best, hair that was more silver than grey tied back in a ponytail. She smiled at Annie with kind eyes. 'Les, what's this? Are we finally allowed to open?'

Annie frowned, but Mr. Fairbrother just chuckled. 'I wouldn't go jumping the gun just yet,' he said. 'This here is Miss Annie Collins, Lord Wilfred's granddaughter. Mistress, this is Diane Jenkins, owner of Diane's Pancake House, one of the best pancake shops in England.'

'Hello,' Annie said. 'Please just call me Annie.'

Diane smiled and put her hands together. 'Annie, dear, welcome to Undercastle, the great lost village of the Lake District. If you're truly Lord Wilfred's successor, then can I make one tiny request?'

Annie shrugged. 'Sure.'

'Can we please, after all these long and lonely years, finally, at long last … open?'

11

LETTERS

'IT WAS THE MOST BIZARRE OF DAYS,' ANNIE SAID, sitting by the window in her guestroom, holding her phone steady in order to keep the signal at three bars. Julie's voice was a little crackly, but Annie could hear just enough. If she really was the heir to this magnificent estate, one of her first commands would be to ask the local telecoms company to put in a decent phone mast.

'So, it's all real, then?'

'It seems like it. This estate really does appear to belong to my family, although I can barely get my head around it. I mean … it's massive. I haven't yet explored the whole house and I found out today that it comes with its own village, complete with actual real life residents.'

'I can't believe it. You're so lucky.'

'I can't believe it either. It feels like a weird dream. Get this though … this whole village, it's like some kind of fairytale place that my grandfather decided to turn into a tourist village, but it seems he's such a perfectionist that he died before he made the decision to open it. It has pubs and restaurants and cake shops and cafés … but none of them are open to the public. There are a hundred or so residents who basically serve each other.'

'So where do they get their money from?'

Annie shook her head, smiling at the memory. 'That's the other thing,' she said. 'Honestly, if I hadn't seen it with my own eyes, I wouldn't have believed it.'

'Come on, spill the beans,' Julie said.

'What's in that big building?' Annie said, pointing at a low stone building at the village's far end, which looked like a warehouse.

'Ah, that's the factory,' Mr. Fairbrother said.

'What kind of factory?'

'They make all sorts.'

'Can we have a look?'

'Well, it's your factory now,' Mr. Fairbrother said.

The entrance was sculptured to look like two colourful toy soldiers, both holding up swords that crossed in the middle, and the double doors were painted gold. Mr. Fairbrother went first, Annie following after.

'Oh, wow.'

Inside, the factory's lobby reminded Annie of the kitchens at Stone Spire Hall. It was all pistons and pipes in bright colours, the way a child might imagine a toy factory or the guts of a giant Christmas robot.

Mr. Fairbrother went up to a red and green striped reception desk and rang a little bell. While he leaned on the counter, Annie wandered over to a set of shelves stacked with all manner of different toys, none of which she had ever seen before. For the most part they were made out of wood and metal, with clockwork cogs and handles giving motion to ornately carved and painted animals and mannequins. She squatted down to pick up one elaborate dog toy from a bottom shelf, which made a clicking bark at the press of its wooden tail. Turning it over, she found a manufacturer's stamp:

Handmade in Wonder Toy Studios,
Undercastle, Lake District
Authentic and Unique
LIMITED EDITION: No. 1
Merry Christmas!

Picking up another doll, she found a similar stamp on its underside. She was just examining another when the door opened behind the counter and a man stepped through. Before Annie could react, he spread his arms and began to sing:

'I welcome you to Wonder Toy,
It's a beautiful day to bring you joy,
Happiness is in our hands,
Welcome to our winter wonderla—'

The man paused, and his wide smile dropped. 'Oh, Les. It's you. For a minute there, I thought—'

Annie stood up, the doll still in her hands. The man stared at her, and Annie stared back, unable to deny a wide smile. He wore a uniform of green and red and a little green hat which had a white bobble that hung down to his shoulders. He had a handlebar moustache flecked with spots of silver glitter. His cheeks glowed—rouge rather than natural—and his eyes were a startling, winter lake blue.

'Are you a real elf?' she asked slowly, putting the doll back on the shelf.

The man stepped back and gave a flourishing bow. 'Of course,' he said. 'Davvie Sprinkle-Toes at your service. It is my pleasure to welcome you to Wonder Toy Studios. Would you like a guided tour?'

Mr. Fairbrother chuckled. 'Nice show, Dave,' he said. 'You'd have made the old lord proud. This is Miss Annie Collins, Lord Wilfred's heir.'

Davvie's—Dave's—smile dropped. 'Oh. Well, Miss Collins, it's lovely to meet you.'

'Call me Annie,' Annie said. 'And it's lovely to meet you too.'

'So, you're Lord Wilf's heir, are you? I wondered what would happen when the old guy popped his clogs. Any chance that we could finally—'

'Open?'

Dave smiled. 'So I'm not the first person you've spoken to, then?'

'I had a talk with Mr. Fairbrother—Les—on the way back,' Annie said to Julie, kicking a stool against the wall by the window and then standing up on it. Checking her phone, she saw the third bar of reception appeared a little steadier. 'It turns out my grandfather was something of an inventor. However, he was also a perfectionist. He had all these grand plans for this place to open as a tourist village, but he never actually did it.'

'How lovely, but how sad at the same time that his dream was never realised.'

'I know. It's bizarre. And when you see it all, it's hard to believe. I mean, the factory, all the staff are dressed like elves. They don't actually seem to mind—it turns out they get paid pretty well and they do a maximum of five hours per shift. And all the cafés and shops are kind of in this weird state of preparation. They only actually serve the village residents, so they're not very busy, and they get to spend their time figuring out the absolute best recipes for everything.' She smiled at the memory. 'I had this caramel and chocolate muffin infused with Christmas spice from a cake shop on the way back, and I literally thought I was going to die, it was so good.'

'Sounds wonderful. How on earth did your grandfather afford it all?'

'Well, I had to ask that, since it's all apparently now mine—which I still can't get my head round, by the way—and there are a few things. Among some boring stuff like investments, they actually do ship out some of the toys that they make, and there's also a brewery that makes Christmas-spiced local liquor. I had a glass of some in the factory and it was divine. Oh, and there's a live-stream from the factory that is super popular. And get this—my grandfather actually has a contract with the Post Office to reply to Christmas letters. Most of the letters kids post to Father Christmas, Lapland or Greenland or The North Pole, end up in an office in grandfather's village where a team of workers dressed as elves sit down and write replies.'

'No!' Julie chuckled on the other end of the line. 'Isn't that a bit of an anti-climax?'

'You'd think, wouldn't you? But they wear elf uniforms and sing Christmas songs as they do it. Makes it feel kind of magical.'

'My kids wrote Christmas letters last year, but they never heard anything back,' Julie said.

'According to one um, elf—he told me his name was Bunty Glitter-bottom, or Brian, if I preferred—they actually have a year delay, which keeps them in business all year round. So the letters they received last Christmas will be returned this year. They literally spend all year replying to last Christmas's letters. Apparently they respond quicker to email—the modern world and all that—but letters are still the preferred method for most little children.'

'It's like a fairytale, isn't it?'

Annie sighed. 'I keep expecting to wake up,' she said. 'I was all ready to put on a pair of elf slippers and do a little jig when Mr. Fairbrother told me I have an appointment with the accountant tomorrow.'

'Puts a dampener on it, doesn't it?'

Annie let out a shrill laugh, then quickly put her hand over her mouth. 'I told him to turn up wearing a Christmas hat,' she said. 'I think there was a little too much liquor in that muffin—' A bell tinkled by the door. Annie looked up. 'Sorry, I've got to go. I just got summoned to dinner.'

They said their goodbyes and Annie hung up. As she put the phone down on the window ledge, she let out a long sigh.

This was incredible. Beyond incredible, it was almost unbelievable. Breathing slowly as she looked out of the window at the distant glitter of moonlight on the lake, she reminded herself what she had once promised if she ever won the National Lottery.

'It won't change me,' she whispered. 'I'll stay the same person that I was before.'

But how did you go about that when you discovered out of the blue that you had inherited a country estate and an entire adjoining village? You felt like you needed to tie weights to your feet to keep yourself grounded. She could click her fingers and demand a unicorn steak for dinner and Mrs. Growell would somehow try to find it. She could order Mr. Fairbrother to trim the privet hedges into a likeness of Michael Jackson and no doubt he'd be out there at dawn tomorrow with his shears.

Three days ago she was turning off her fridge with the dodgy non-closing door to save electricity. It would be easy to forget.

She went over to the bed, pulled on a jumper, and headed downstairs.

12

DEFROSTING

'GOOD EVENING, MISTRESS,' MRS. GROWELL GREETED Annie, as she reached the bottom of the stairs. A fire flickered in the grate of the entrance hall, Annie's table set up just near enough to keep it warm.

Annie gave a sheepish smile, having not seen Mrs. Growell since the flour incident this morning.

'I'm sorry,' she muttered.

Mrs. Growell gave a slight tilt of her head in acknowledgement. 'This evening's menu is on your table. We will begin with oxtail soup, followed by roasted pheasant, and for dessert we have caramel ribbon infused meringue. Would you like cheese or cured ham as a side dish?'

'Ah … cheese?'

Mrs. Growell gave a respectful nod. 'Understood. Please take a seat and I will be with you shortly.'

Annie sat down. The chair and table had been carefully placed for the fire to keep her warm, but not too warm. Lamps lit in alcoves around the high-ceilinged room provided a peaceful ambience. There was only one thing missing.

Company.

Annie had left her phone upstairs, because there was nowhere on the ground floor where she could get a signal. A video call with Julie would make her feel much better, but that was out. She got up and went to a nearby bookshelf, but it was all history books or dusty classics, and nothing took her fancy. With a sigh she found herself pining for the dog-eared twisty thrillers that she bought from the secondhand shop in the arcade, and wondered if they were yet another of the things that identified her as a pauper. Among this grandiosity and wealth, she was beginning to feel a little out of place.

She was just wondering whether it might be worth trying to decipher the first paragraph or two of a Dickens or Austen when the front door opened and Mr. Fairbrother came in, wrapped briefly in a theatrical flurry of snow before he closed the door behind him. Shaking snow off his jacket onto the mat, he pulled off his boots and hung his jacket up on a hook by the door. Then, coming through the second door to the entrance hall which Mrs. Growell had left propped open, he raised a hand in greeting.

'Good evening, Mistress,' he said, cheeks flushed from the cold, little lumps of snow caught in his hair starting to melt and dribble down his face. 'Goodness, is it dinner time already? I suppose I'd better head into the dragon's lair and see what she can rustle up.'

As he turned to go, Annie put up a hand. 'Ah … Les? Mr. Fairbrother … would you mind, uh, joining me for dinner?'

Mr. Fairbrother frowned. 'What, you mean, eat together? Well, I don't know … Lord Wilf liked his time alone with his thoughts and his books—'

'I'm not Lord Wilf. And to be honest, I'd practically kill for some conversation. Look, there's a chair over there. I'll sort everything out while you go down to the kitchens. And while you're at it, can you ask Mrs. Growell to come up too?'

Mr. Fairbrother's eyes widened. 'You want me to call her up here? I mean, I can ask her, but I wouldn't hold up much hope. Pretty set in her ways, she is.'

'Just ask her. Look, three days ago I was dirt poor. I could barely afford a bus ticket and one of my shoe laces was a piece of string. I mean, my jogging shoes—my work shoes are slip-ons—but you get the idea. And I find out I'm the heir to this … empire? I just can't turn into some aristocratic landowner with a click of my fingers. I just want to be … normal.'

Mr. Fairbrother chuckled. 'All right. I'll ask her. But don't get your hopes up.'

He headed downstairs. Annie got up, went out into the hall where a couple of spare chairs were tucked into alcoves, and carried them back over to the table laid out with her cutlery. She moved her knives and forks—there were three of each; she couldn't help but smile—and slid the little tablecloth into the table's centre. She had just sat down when two figures appeared on the kitchen stairs.

Mr. Fairbrother, holding a tray in each hand, wore a wide grin. Mrs. Growell, standing a little beside him with a tray in her hands, looked like someone had asked her to dance a jig, her face fraught with discomfort.

Mr. Fairbrother set down a cheese sandwich across the table from Annie, then laid a tray in front of Annie with a bowl of oxtail soup and a crusty bread roll. A nub of butter sat in a small serving dish. With a long, contented sigh, he pulled out a chair and sat down, then waved Mrs. Growell forward.

'Come on, Marge. Don't be shy. Mistress's orders.'

Mrs. Growell approached slowly, setting another cheese sandwich down on the table in front of a place to Annie's left. Then, from another tray she took a decanter of wine and set it in front of Annie.

'We need a couple more glasses,' Annie said.

Mrs. Growell's stern visage slipped briefly with a raised eyebrow quickly pulled back into place. 'I don't drink … on duty.'

'Come on, Marge, just a sip,' Mr. Fairbrother said with a chuckle, getting up and fetching a couple of glasses out of a cabinet near the wall. As he came back to the table, he wiped one on his shirt then blew dust out of the other. As Mrs. Growell stared, horrified, he set the first down in front of him and the second in front of her. As he settled into his seat, she reached out and switched them around.

Annie picked up a spoon and smiled. 'Isn't this better? Although, I have to say, that cheese sandwich looks pretty nice.'

'Locally produced cheddar,' Mrs. Growell said in a quiet, taut voice. 'My … favourite.'

'Do you mind if I swap?'

Before Mrs. Growell was forced into an awkward reply, Mr. Fairbrother chuckled. 'You can have half of mine, Mistress,' he said. 'Although you keep your soup. After that walk we had today, you'll need it.'

'What about you?'

'Ah, I always double down on pudding. And there might be a bit of leftover from that pheasant.'

'I insist that we share it together,' Annie said, glancing at Mrs. Growell to see her reaction. Mrs. Growell, however, was staring across the table at the empty chair on the other side.

'Who … is that for?'

'It's for Isabella,' Annie said. 'You know, the girl who no one talks about who I'm pretty sure locked me out on the balcony, is hiding the keys, and who runs away every time I try to talk to her.'

Mrs. Growell frowned. 'Isabella….'

'Will she be joining us?'

Mr. Fairbrother, wearing a nervous pout, looked from Annie to Mrs. Growell. 'Marge?'

'I believe the girl has dined already,' Mrs. Growell said, still staring at the chair.

'That's too bad. Maybe tomorrow?'

'Maybe.'

'Oh well.' Annie gave a sheepish smile. 'Shall we tuck in, then?'

'Tuck in….'

Mr. Fairbrother put his hands together. 'I'll say grace.' Then, with a chuckle, he said, 'Grace,' again, then picked up his sandwich and took a huge bite, pieces of grated cheddar dropping all over his plate.

Mrs. Growell rolled her eyes. 'Oh, Les. You're impossible….'

13

OPEN FOR BUSINESS

'Did you manage to get the pole out of the housekeeper's arse?' Julie asked, chuckling, as Annie stood on the stool by the window, the phone pressed against her ear as snow fell gently outside.

'I'd say it was a partial removal,' Annie said. 'I couldn't get her to drink more than a couple of sips of wine, because she insisted that she was still on duty. She did laugh at one of the caretaker's jokes, though. Well, it was more of a humph than a real laugh, but she did at least smile.'

'And have you decided what to do?'

'I'm still trying to figure it all out. No one can find a key to my grandfather's suite anywhere. I'm thinking of just taking the door off its hinges or abseiling down to the window from the roof.'

'You don't know what's inside?'

'Apparently his rooms were strictly off limits.'

'He sounds like a bit of a prude.'

'To be quite honest, I'm not sure what to think about him. I tried to call Mum again, but she's gone on a polar bear viewing expedition to the Northwest Territories and is going to be off the grid for the next few weeks.'

'You must feel like you're living in a TV show.'

'Something like that. It'll all come crashing down in a few days when I have to go back to work.'

'You're not surely going back to the bank?'

'To be honest, I don't know what to do. I feel like a fish out of water. Everything is totally awkward. At least back home I felt in some control.'

Even as she said it, she wondered if it was true. In control enough to pay her electric bill? In control enough to stop crazy customers from attacking her?

'You know what I think?'

'What?'

'You should just roll with it. Enjoy it for what it is, and see what happens. And if you're feeling guilty about it, you could always open it up for disadvantaged kids or something like that.'

Annie nodded. 'You're right. Maybe I will.'

'I'd better go. I've got to get the kids ready for school. What's on the agenda for today?'

'I have a meeting with the village council about opening the village to tourists, and after that I'm going to try to find the girl who seems to live here, whom nobody wants to talk about.'

'Well, good luck. I'm going to get the kids off to school, then go to the dentist, then nip to Superdrug because we're one upset stomach away from running out of toilet roll. Have a nice day, Lady Collins.'

Annie smiled. 'I'll try.'

Meeting the town council was easier than she had

expected. Ten representatives, some from the local businesses, others elected by the other townsfolk, met her in a community hall near the train station. Annie was delighted to find a spread of mince pies and fudge had been laid out, along with a large jug of hot chocolate.

'So,' she said, brow beaded with sweat, hands shaking with nerves, as she stood in front of the seated council members, 'thanks for coming today. My name's Annie Collins, so please call me Annie, not Mistress, or Lady, or anything else high and mighty. You might have noticed that I have no clue what I'm doing—'

'You're doing fine, dear,' said Diane Jenkins, sitting at the front with her hands folded over her knees.

'Ah, thanks. Well, I'm still figuring out what's going on here, but it seems like my grandfather was assembling some kind of Christmas village, but hadn't actually got around to opening it to the public.'

'For the past twenty years!' came a frustrated grunt from a rotund man sitting at the back. Somehow, the fact that he was dressed as an elf made him even scarier.

'Well, from what I've seen, it looks pretty good to me, so as, ah, manager—'

'Owner,' Mr. Fairbrother said from where he sat near the wall. 'You're the owner, ah … Mistress.'

'Okay, so, owner then … as owner, I'd like to authorise the opening of the village. If, you know, that's something that you all want, and it's something that's possible.'

'Just gotta remove the NO ENTRY sign from the access road and stick an ad in the paper,' said another elf. 'We've been waiting for this moment forever. Every year Lord Collins was just, "soon, soon, soon" … keeping us all on hold while locking himself up like some Christmas hat-wearing Howard Hughes.'

After the meeting was over, Mr. Fairbrother gave Annie a wide smile. 'You're a natural, Mistress,' he said.

'I have no idea what I'm doing,' she admitted, wiping her face with a tissue.

'Well, just hang around the village for a while, get to know a few people. It'll get easier in time.'

He made his excuses—apparently one of the reindeer had got into a private garden—and left. Annie helped herself to one leftover mince pie, then went outside.

The morning's snow had melted off the streets, but still lay on top of bushes and stone walls, turning the village into a giant Christmas cake. Annie wandered around for a while, becoming familiar with the place, before the lingering cold got the better of her and she headed for Diane's Pancake House for an afternoon snack and a bit of warmth.

'Hello, Annie dear,' Diane Jenkins greeted her. 'How are you settling in?'

Annie had quickly warmed to Diane, who felt more like a grandparent than any of her biological ones ever had. She shook her head and shrugged.

'Getting there, I suppose.'

'You're not finding this easy, are you?'

'Not at all. I'm supposed to be happy, aren't I? The poor girl that wins the lottery? I mean, this is most people's idea of a dream come true, isn't it?'

Dianne poured two cups of coffee out of a filter, came out from behind the counter and took them to a table.

'Sit down, dear. It looks like you need a rest.'

'Thanks.'

Diane slid a pot of creamers and sugar sticks across the table. 'You can build a lot of things with money,' she said. 'Castles, towers, entire towns. But you can't build a human soul.' She chuckled. 'Not that anyone ever told Wilfred that.'

'What do you mean?'

'I'm getting the impression that you don't know much about your grandfather.'

'I haven't seen him since I was a child, and until last week I thought he died twenty-odd years ago. My father died pretty young, but before he passed, he never spoke about him. And my mother, if she knows anything, isn't saying.'

Diane gave a wistful smile. 'Your grandfather was a unique man,' she said. 'But also a troubled one. Before he started to shut himself away from the world, we used to talk. You see, my family grew up in Undercastle, back when it was just a quiet, uninteresting village. I knew your grandfather when he was young, in fact he was only a couple of years older than me.' She gave a long sigh. 'He was so ambitious. Came first in all the tests, won all of the competitions. However, he was also a dreamer. And I think in the end he dreamed too big.'

'How do you mean?'

'Well, everything you see around you was his creation. This village was supposed to be his magical gift to the world, a holiday village of joy and excitement. He hired the best craftsmen, the best chefs, the best entertainers … and then we waited. And waited. And … waited.' Diane grinned and tapped her wrist. 'All we wanted to do was open up to the world, but he wouldn't allow it. He was waiting for that extra something….'

'Which was?'

Diane sighed. 'No one's quite sure. But the years went by, and I for one got extremely good at making pancakes.' She shook her head and chuckled. 'For the fifteen or so local residents that stop by each day.'

'Everything about this place is so mysterious.' Annie sighed. 'I mean, why was Grandfather estranged from my family? I've always thought he died when I was in school. No one ever mentioned him. I mean … wouldn't my family have known he had all this?'

'People can be very secretive,' Diane said. 'And you'd be surprised what can be hidden in plain sight.'

Annie smiled. 'That's true. I'm not even sure how many people live in the house over there. There's Mrs. Growell, and Mr. Fairbrother … and the ghost.'

Diane gave a knowing nod. 'You're talking about Isabella, aren't you? Now, there's a story. One I can't tell well. Perhaps Margaret … if you can defrost her a little.'

'What do you mean?'

'Everything was different after Isabella arrived.'

'When did she arrive?'

Diane shrugged. 'It must have been twenty years ago now. Everything changed after that.'

'You mean … she was born here?'

'Oh, nothing like that, dear.' Diane lifted her coffee cup, took a sip, and gazed off into space. 'She blew in, on a storm.'

14

INVESTIGATIONS

Annie couldn't help but smile as she watched Mrs. Growell scooping small spoonfuls of cornflakes onto a teaspoon. Each was lifted to her mouth in turn, given a resentful frown, and then passed through lips parted barely wide enough to allow them. Then, a couple of barely perceptible crunches later, the spoon would drop for another load.

Beside her, Mr. Fairbrother shared none of her awkwardness, crunching happily on a bacon sandwich as he read a local newspaper balanced on one leg crossed over the other. Annie, with a spread in front of her of muesli, toast, and sliced fruit, looked from one to the other with a growing sense of satisfaction.

'Isn't this nice?' she said. 'So much better to eat in company than alone, don't you think?'

Mrs. Growell's face tightened. 'Company ... is overrated.'

'Marge, you seen this?' Mr. Fairbrother said, oblivious to Mrs. Growell's awkwardness. 'Got a sale on curtains over in Drapery Warehouse this weekend. Those old rags in your quarters down there could do with an upgrade, eh?'

Mrs. Growell closed her eyes briefly as though hoping the world would disappear.

Annie just grinned. 'Why don't you two take the day off and go and look? Perhaps I could cook dinner for you instead?'

'I am employed as a housekeeper,' Mrs. Growell said quietly. 'Therefore, I housekeep.'

'Come on, Marge, Mistress is offering you a day off.'

'Please just call me Annie,' Annie said. 'It's so much better to be on first name terms, isn't it, Mar ... uh, Mrs. Growell?'

'Delightful.'

'Will ... ah, Isabella be joining us for breakfast?' Annie asked, nodding at the empty space between herself and Mr. Fairbrother. 'I'd really like to get to know her. And ... you know, find out where she's hidden all the keys.'

'I believe the girl has eaten,' Mrs. Growell said.

'So ... what does she do around here?' Annie asked, probing for a chink in Mrs. Growell's armour. The housekeeper gave a shudder, however, as though rattled by a sudden wind.

It was Mr. Fairbrother who answered. 'Not a lot,' he said. 'I suppose you'd call her the chambermaid what with all them costumes she likes wearing, but without much in the way of chambers needing attending, she pretty much just does her own thing.'

'Mr. Fairbrother, it's uncouth to speak of those outside one's presence,' Mrs. Growell said, as tightlipped as ever, although briefly lowering her façade long enough to take a sip of coffee and then wince at its perceived bitterness.

'Come on, Marge, if that were the case, the girl might just disappear.'

'I heard she arrived on a storm,' Annie said.

Mr. Fairbrother chuckled. Mrs. Growell set down her coffee cup with a hard thump, her face tighter than ever. Annie wondered if a little whisky slipped into the coffee pot might help loosen her up a little.

'I should clear the breakfast things,' Mrs. Growell said.

'I can help you—'

'No!' Mrs. Growell put up a hand, then immediately looked regretful. Her face softened a little, and she almost —but not quite—smiled. 'You have things to do, Mistress … Annie. I … insist.'

'Sure.'

Annie at least managed to stack her plates into a single pile before Mrs. Growell scooped them up, set them on a tray, and headed off to the kitchens, throwing one last sour look in Mr. Fairbrother's direction as she left. The moment she had gone through the door into the entrance hall and disappeared down the stairs to the kitchens, Mr. Fairbrother folded his newspaper over and sat up.

'Wow, did you see that? It was like a glacier calving or whatever. Forty years she served Lord Wilf and I never heard her say his first name.'

'Why won't anyone talk about Isabella?' Annie said, turning to Mr. Fairbrother. 'It's like it's bad luck to mention her name.'

Mr. Fairbrother put his newspaper on the table and turned to face her. 'That girl … she's a bit of a mystery to the lot of us, you see. You're reet, she came in on a storm —well, just after … I suppose you'd say it left her behind. It was a shocker, took half the tiles off the roof, it did. Scared the hair off my head getting up there to put them back. You know what they say? 'Twas a dark and stormy night….'

'And Isabella just … appeared?'

'Knock came on the door as we was getting ready to retire for the night. Was just clearing out the fire. Marge was down in the kitchen, and your grandfather was in his chair, reading some book or other. Knock came on the door and when we went to look, was only a baby there, wrapped up in a blanket, set inside this wicker basket. Clutched in her hand was a butterfly.'

'A real one?'

Mr. Fairbrother laughed. 'No, some plastic rattle thing. No idea what happened to it. The girl canna have been more than six months old. Pretty little thing.'

'Did you find out where she came from?'

Mr. Fairbrother shook his head. 'See, here's the funny thing. Girl was in the crib there, and it was snowing out, drifting pretty deep, but there weren't no line of tracks in the snow. Not one. As if she appeared by magic.'

'That's unbelievable.'

'Yeah, we was a little surprised, that's for sure. Asked around the village the next day, but no one knew owt. Went further afield, even called the police, but nowt. In the end, your grandfather chose to bring her up as his own.'

Annie's eyes widened. 'What?'

'Well, 'twas Mrs. Growell who did most of the mothering, if you could believe it. Down in her chambers beside the kitchen. Your grandfather was quite taken with her, though. Seems like he felt he'd not done too good a job first time around, so decided to make up for it.'

'He raised her as his own daughter?'

Mr. Fairbrother shrugged. 'Kind of. But … ah, it's hard to explain. Better if you meet her, then you'll see.'

'I've tried, but it's nearly impossible to find her. In which wing of the house are her rooms? Or does she live with Mrs. Growell?'

'Ah, not anymore. You see, that's just it. She doesn't actually live here in the house.'

'Where does she live, then?'

Mr. Fairbrother rubbed his knees and stood up. With a grunt and a quick rub of his back, he walked over to the nearest window.

'Out there,' he said, nodding. 'In the forest.'

15

THE KEY TO EVERYTHING

ANOTHER PIECE OF THE JIGSAW HAD FIT INTO PLACE, BUT there were still so many missing. In search of another, after breakfast Annie left Mr. Fairbrother to clear snow from the back courtyard and headed out to Undercastle.

The forest was beautiful and pristine with its fresh blanket of snow. Annie took a deep breath, feeling the cool air in her lungs, marvelling at the vastness of the nature around her. A bird darted through the trees, startling her, and reindeer tracks crisscrossed the path.

But were they really the tracks of the reindeer? Could one set be the tracks of a girl, slipping from the house back into the forest?

Mr. Fairbrother's revelation about Isabella had only raised more questions. Mrs. Growell, who had apparently acted as the girl's de facto mother, probably had more of the answers, but getting them out of her would be like chipping fossils out of ancient rock. Maybe … with enough time.

In the meantime, though, Annie's grandfather's secrets would be more easily yielded … with the right tools.

In the village, Annie headed to the Wonder Toy Studios and asked for Dave Wilson.

'Davvy Sprinkle-Toes at your service,' Dave said, giving Annie a flourishing bow. 'Lovely to see you again so soon. What can I help you with?'

Annie frowned. 'I'm looking for some kind of tool. I need to break into my grandfather's suite.'

'And you don't have a key?'

'It appears both the original and several spares have gone missing.'

'That's too bad.' With a grin, Dave opened a drawer behind the counter and lifted up a heavy object. 'May I suggest a hammer?'

'I was thinking of something more subtle. You know, to pick the lock? You guys are specialists, aren't you? You must have something I can use … or at least be able to make something.'

Dave grinned. 'I'm sure we can come up with something. Give us half an hour. In the meantime, why don't you take a wander, get some coffee or something?'

'Sure.'

Annie left Dave to his work and wandered up the street. She hoped to stop in and see Diane, whom she'd taken a liking for, but the pancake house was closed with a sign on the window saying OUT TO (A VERY LARGE) LUNCH.

A little further along was Frank's Fudge, which she'd not yet visited. As she pushed through the door, a little tinkle of Christmas music sounded and a delicious sugary smell wafted out.

'Well, hello,' came a voice from a kitchen behind the counter, and a moment later a middle-aged man with a kind smile appeared, wiped his hands on a towel, and leaned on the counter. 'Miss Collins, it's lovely to have your business. Everything is on the house for you, of course.'

Annie smiled. 'Literally charged to the house account?'

'Of course.'

'Then I'll have a large fudge sundae with extra whipped cream. Actually, can I have two, and can you put them in boxes for me to take back? They're for Mrs. Growell and Mr. Fairbrother. Actually, I've got a couple of places where I want to stop and say hello, so could you have someone run them up to the hall for me?'

'Got a young lad who helps me out. Sure he wouldn't mind,' Frank said. 'And for yourself?'

'I'll have a solitary cube of low fat, low cholesterol, zero sugar, plain fudge, please.'

'So … an empty plate?'

'Sod it. Give me a fat chunk of whatever it is you're cooking. And do you do coffee?'

'Of course.'

'And a large one of those, please.'

'Coming right up.'

As Frank got to work, Annie smiled again. 'By the way, why are you wearing a Christmas hat?'

Frank chuckled. 'Well, I heard that thanks to your graceful kindness, we're finally going to get some customers. You know, I've been living here ten years, getting paid a stupid amount of money, and all I've ever done is package my fudge up in boxes and watch it loaded into the backs of lorries. I'm sure there are people all over the country enjoying it, but I don't get to see it. And there's nothing better than fresh fudge. As soon as you package it up, the flavour starts to fade. What made you decide to overrule your grandfather's law and open the village at long last?'

Annie shrugged. 'I've never been in charge of anything

before,' she said. 'I work in a rubbish bank job where I get verbally—and occasionally physically—abused by customers who can't get loans or mortgages or overdrafts, and the main word in my vocabulary is "no". No to this, no to that. No, no, no. And then I come here, and I get told I'm in charge of everything. And look at this place. Who wouldn't want everyone to visit it? It's just lovely. I didn't know my grandfather at all, but I'm starting to think he was crazy.'

Frank gave a nervous chuckle. 'He was certainly unique. You know, we all miss the old guy because he was friendly enough, but we're craftsmen, artisans. I've spent twenty years perfecting fudge recipes, and I left a successful business in Edinburgh to come here, on the promise that I was moving to a bustling tourist village where thousands of people would get to enjoy my fudge. So … when do we finally open?'

Annie smiled. 'On Saturday.' She couldn't help but giggle as she remembered a meeting with the station master yesterday. Diane, introducing them, had referred to the rotund man in the black top hat as Bill, but he had introduced himself to Annie as Willy Whistle, Station Master. 'Um … Mr. Whistle said the Undercastle Line has been checked and cleared to resume service, so the first load of tourists should be arriving in the afternoon. Will you be ready?'

Frank spread his arms and looked behind him at a glass display case filled with delicious fudge. 'I'm ready now,' he said. Then, picking up a plate overloaded with chunks of freshly baked fudge in a rainbow of different colours, he handed it to Annie and said, 'However, fudge is best when it's fresh, so let's not go wasting any. You get stuck in, and I'll bring your coffee in a sec.'

Annie stared at the fudge, her nose going crazy with

the aromas of chocolate, marshmallow, caramel, cinnamon and others she couldn't place. She looked up at Frank and grinned.

'I think I'm going to pass out,' she said. 'But I'll see how much I can eat first.'

Half an hour later, feeling a couple of pounds heavier but several degrees happier, Annie staggered back to the Wonder Toy Studios, absently wondering whether Undercastle had a dentist, and if not, whether she should see if they could hire one. It might prove necessary for anyone staying longer than a couple of days.

Dave was waiting for her behind the reception desk. As Annie came in, he looked up and smiled.

'Ah, there you are. Did you survive?'

Annie patted her stomach. 'Just about. I think I'll need to take the scenic route back if I want to have any space left for dinner.'

Dave chuckled. 'The one via Scotland?'

'That's it.'

'Well, if you do make it back, this should help.' With a triumphant grin, Dave reached under the counter and lifted up a small pine box, the wood washed with blue paint. Holding it out to Annie, he slid a cover out of grooves in the top to reveal a gold key sitting on a bed of diced pine cones. Despite the lavish packaging, the key was large and chunky, far too big to open any of the locks in Stone Spire Hall, not least the one on her grandfather's door, which was much smaller.

'Ah … that's wonderful, but I'm not sure—'

'This,' Dave said, 'is a magic key. Capable of opening any lock, anywhere.'

'Are you sure?'

'Trust me.'

'Well, what about this cabinet? That takes a key.'

Dave shook his head. 'This key only opens doors.'

'You said it opens everything.'

Dave gave a sheepish grin. 'Well, that's the blurb on the packet, isn't it?'

'So it won't open my grandfather's door?'

'Oh, it definitely will.'

'But what if it doesn't?'

Dave spread his hands. 'Look, here's my promise. If it doesn't open that door, come right back here, and I'll give you a refund.'

'I didn't pay anything!'

'Nothing ventured, nothing gained. Look, if it really doesn't work, I'll buy you a fudge lunch. As much fudge as you can eat, and as much coffee as you can drink.'

'Do I get whipped cream?'

'Of course.'

'I'd still prefer it if this key worked.'

'Just trust me.'

Annie wasn't sure whether Dave was pranking her or not, but even so, the key looked nice. If it didn't have any function at all, it would still make a nice Christmas present for someone.

After wandering around the village for a little while longer, meeting a few more local people and ducking into a few of the quaint shops which sold everything from homemade hats to garden ornaments, she headed back to Stone Spire Hall, determined to finally get some answers.

Evening was already approaching, the sun low in the sky, leaving patches of snow that hadn't melted away glittering with orange and yellow, with the lake in the distance brightest of all. Annie was almost relieved by the shadows under the trees as she followed the forest path back towards the house. Much of the snow here still remained, and she passed several lines of animal tracks most likely belonging to the reindeer. She glanced nervously into the trees, wondering if the animals would come to inspect her again, promising herself not to panic if they did.

Then, not far from the house, a line of tracks crossed the path that were too large for reindeer.

Annie stopped. Too small for Mr. Fairbrother's boots, they were nevertheless clearly belonging to shoes of some kind. Narrow at the front, with the heels leaving flattened circles, Annie imagined Cinderella fleeing from the ball in glass slippers, only this time it had been snowing and she had managed not to lose one.

The line of tracks led into the trees. With barely a hesitation, Annie stepped off the path and began to follow.

16

THE COTTAGE IN THE WOODS

FOR THE FIRST FEW STEPS, ANNIE WAS TRUDGING through snow and the pine needles buried beneath, and began to fear that she might get lost. Then, almost without warning, she stepped down onto a clearly marked forest trail, and realised that the owner of the tracks had merely been lazy, cutting off the corner of the trail that wound through the trees before joining up with the main path a little further ahead. Following the tracks, however, Annie headed deeper into the forest.

The path wound gently uphill. A couple of times it reached intersections with other paths, where wooden signposts and maps directed her to waterfalls, lookout points, an orchard, and even a picnic area. In a few places, where the snow had partially melted, Annie thought she had lost the tracks, only to find them a little further along, the person she was tracking having ignored all of the signs to follow a single main path which had no markings.

Then, just as it was getting almost too dark to see anything, Annie came to a chain hanging across the path with NO ENTRY carved in ornate letters and painted gold.

Perhaps the most passive no entry sign Annie had ever seen, she duly stepped over the chain and continued on, reminding herself that she was still technically on her newly acquired property and therefore exempt from any trespassing rules. Plus, it was getting dark, and she really hoped that the forest would soon give way to somewhere a little more open. She had been heading gently uphill the whole way, and at least knew she only had to go back downhill and walk in a generally straight direction, but she could barely see the path in front of her, and had neglected to bring any kind of torch.

And then, like a miracle, she spotted lights through the trees.

With each step, more lights appeared, until a ring of them were visible, stretching off to either side through the trees.

Christmas lights, strung through the lower branches of the trees, just above Annie's head. She stepped beneath them, then, as her eyes adjusted to the dark, she found herself at the edge of a clearing. A little picket fence encircled a garden, rose bushes and azaleas now speckled with fresh snow. A gate opened onto a cobblestone path, which led through flowerbeds to a front step, and a door, and a quaint, picturesque cottage, stone-walled, its dormer windows set in alcoves, its roofing eaves overhanging a porch. Lights pressed at curtains pulled across the windows.

Annie had no choice but to approach the door. The stars had come out through a break in the trees overhead, but the forest was black, the world disappeared beyond the line of Christmas lights. If there was no one home, she thought she might just sit down on the porch and wait for morning, rather than brave the forest in the dark.

She gave the knocker a little tap.

'Hello? Is anyone in there? It's Annie from Stone Spire Hall. I'm afraid I got a little lost in the woods, and I saw your lights….'

For a few seconds, nothing happened. Annie was just about to try again when the door creaked. Annie stepped back as it opened a crack, and warm light flooded out onto the step. A face appeared, its features in shadow. What had Annie been expecting? A terrifying witch, perhaps with a cooking pot on a stove bubbling somewhere in the background?

Without a word, the face moved back, and the door opened wider.

'Isabella?'

The girl was dressed in a red, hooded cloak, but at least wasn't carrying a basket full of pies or apples. She stepped back, lowering her head.

'Can I come in?'

Isabella nodded. 'Okay,' she said in a quiet, mouselike voice.

She stepped back from the door, holding it open for Annie, who stepped inside, then waited on a mat in a little porch while Isabella closed the door.

'Should I take off my boots?' Annie asked.

'Okay,' Isabella said again.

Annie felt a little self-conscious as she reached down to pull off her boots. Isabella watched her the whole time, one hand on her chin like an inquisitive child. Only when Annie nearly tripped while pulling off the second boot did the ice finally break, Isabella letting out a childlike giggle.

'You live here?' Annie asked.

Isabella nodded. 'Yes.'

'I'm sorry to intrude. I got … ah … lost.'

Isabella nodded again, then her eyes widened. 'Tea?'

Annie smiled. 'Tea would be very nice right now.'

The girl turned and scampered off through an arched opening into a tiny kitchen, leaving Annie standing in the hall. She let out a sigh of relief. While she wasn't sure quite what world she had stepped into, at least it was nice to be out of the dark and cold.

Isabella's house appeared to have been built for someone small. It was delightfully traditional, with stone walls, a little fire burning in a hearth, alcoves along the walls filled with vases of dried flowers, and quaint, chandelier-like lights that left everything slightly dim. Isabella had already decorated for Christmas, from the beautiful tree standing in one corner to handmade paper chains all around the walls, to fairy lights strung across the mantelpiece, and models of reindeer and traditional, green-garbed Father Christmases standing on the shelves.

Behind the Christmas decorations, though, it appeared Isabella lived a kind of adult childhood, with the shelves laden with traditional and vintage toys, as well as several Annie had seen displayed in the Wonder Toy Studios reception area. There was no television, but there were shelves and shelves of books, almost entirely children's picture books or young adult series.

'Tea.'

Annie jumped, almost dropping the book she had plucked out of the nearest shelf, a deluxe first edition hardback of *The Gruffalo* that was signed by both the author and illustrator. She put the book back quickly and turned around.

Isabella stood behind her, holding a tray of tea and homemade biscuits, each decorated with chocolate drops arranged in Christmas tree shapes. The girl had lowered her hood, and gave a shy smile.

Annie stared. Isabella had tucked her hair behind one dainty, delicate ear, which rose to a sharp point.

Isabella lifted an eyebrow and smiled. 'Tea?'

'Uh … thank you.'

She sat down at a table and waited while Isabella arranged a cup of tea and the plate of biscuits in front of her, then sat down opposite and cupped her chin with her hands, her eyes watching Annie. She still wore the fairytale red cloak, and set against the cottage's backdrop, Annie wondered if she'd actually stepped inside the pages of one of the storybooks that lined the shelves. All it would need was for a wolf to knock on the door, or Father Christmas to slide down the chimney.

'You live here?' Annie asked again, when it became clear that Isabella wasn't going to start any kind of conversation.

'Yes. Grandfather built it … for me.'

Her voice was bright like a songbird but frail, as though every word could possibly be her last, and ought to be savoured as such.

'Uh, Grandfather? You mean … Lord Wilfred?'

'Grandfather, yes.'

'He's my grandfather too.'

Isabella nodded. 'I know.'

Annie remembered what she had heard about Isabella being left on the steps of Stone Spire Hall as a baby. She guessed that "Grandfather" was as good a label as any to be used by a girl brought up by a man already of retirement age. It made her feel a little ache in her heart, though. Why had he disappeared from her life? Something must have happened between him and her father, but what?

Her dad had been kind but aloof at times. A practical man, he had worked hard without fuss, providing for his family with little fanfare until his unexpected death. When Annie thought back on her childhood, though, he had always been a little standoffish when it came to anything creative or expressive. Her mother had done all the bedtime stories, helped with the art projects, played the games. Her father had been there for every Christmas, but Annie's memory of him was of a man sitting in a chair, watching the afternoon film on TV with a glass of beer in his hand and a look on his face that suggested he would enjoy the day more when it was over.

Had her father fallen out with her grandfather, who had clearly lived a life of expression and celebration, their relationship souring to the point that they had become estranged?

Isabella was still watching her, eyes darting about as though trying to memorise every line and blemish. 'Ah … did my grandfather ever talk about me?'

Isabella's face suddenly broke into a beaming smile, and for the first time Annie felt that the girl might actually be real.

'Oh yes,' she said. 'All the time.'

'Really? What did he say?'

Isabella tilted her head. 'Everything,' she said. 'More tea?'

Annie hadn't even touched the first cup yet, but after Isabella's prompt, she lifted the cup and took a sip.

'It's nice.'

'Thanks.'

'So … ah, you work at Stone Spire Hall?'

'Yes.'

'And you grew up there?'

'Yes.'

'With Mrs. Growell and Mr. Fairbrother and Grandfather?'

Isabella nodded. A small smile spread across her lips. 'Grandfather, Aunt Margaret, and Uncle Les.'

For some reason, Annie found herself chuckling. 'That must have been quite the childhood.'

Isabella smiled. 'Yes.'

'Did you go to school?'

Isabella nodded. 'Undercastle.'

'They have a school?'

'Yes.'

Annie couldn't believe that Undercastle had enough people to have a school, but she decided to take Isabella's word for it. However, there were other mysteries to be solved first.

'Do you know what happened to the key to my grandfather's suite?' Annie asked. 'I've been here several days but I've been unable to get into his private rooms. I'm pretty sure that some of the questions I have will be answered once I can get in there, but right now I'm stuck. I mean, I went to Undercastle this morning and they gave me a key, but I can't see how it would open anything.'

She lifted the paper bag Dave had given her and took out the wooden box. Isabella's eyes immediately lit up as she leaned forward. Then, when Annie opened the box to reveal the key, Isabella let out a little gasp.

'He made it! Does it work?'

Faced with such sudden garrulous enthusiasm from a girl for whom hitherto a three-word sentence had been an event worth celebrating, Annie was initially speechless. Then, as Isabella reached out and lifted the key from the box with delicate fingers that might have graced a harp or violin, Annie said, 'Have you seen one before?'

Isabella gave an enthusiastic nod. 'Yes, yes.'

And before Annie could take another sip of her tea, Isabella stood up, the key held like a newborn kitten in her hands, and hurried out of the room.

Annie waited for a few seconds, but Isabella didn't return. Wondering how the girl could seemingly disappear in such a small house, she took another sip of her tea, a bite of one of the biscuits—which was really quite good—then got up to follow.

The door out of the little living room led into an equally little kitchen, a smaller—but quieter—version of the kitchen at Stone Spire Hall, but Isabella was nowhere to be seen. Annie went back out into the hall, where a staircase rose to an upper floor. She called Isabella's name, then put a hand on the wooden banister and began to climb, her footfalls creaking on the steps. At the top were three doors, each with a wooden sign hanging on a string. One said, *Bathroom*, and a second said *Isabella's Room*, which made Annie smile. The third, rather surprisingly, said *Workshop*. A line of light came from under the door, so Annie approached and gave a little knock.

No one answered, so Annie gently tried the door knob and found the door unlocked. She cracked the door a little and found herself entering a room that was far larger than she might have expected. It was brightly lit, and smelled of wood and glue. In the centre was a large work desk, at which Isabella now sat, while around it was an Aladdin's Cave of half-finished toys, some piled in the boxes, others hanging from strings from the ceiling.

Isabella looked up and smiled. 'Look,' she said, waving Annie forward. 'It works.'

On the desk she had set a large wooden box. As Annie

approached, she realised it was some kind of safety box, perhaps for jewellery. In the middle was a little lock. Isabella took the key Dave had made and held it in her hands. Then, with a wide grin, she tapped it three times against the front of the jewellery box.

A tingle of music filled the air, then a sharp click came from inside the box. Isabella set down the key, then took the box and lifted the lid. She looked up at Annie and smiled. 'See? It works.'

Annie frowned. 'Did you just open that just by tapping it with that key?'

Isabella nodded. 'Yes.'

Annie felt a strange tickle run through her, as though there was some kind of magic in the room. 'Uh … how?'

'Magic.'

'Magic?'

Isabella grinned again. 'Kind of. Resonance.' She held up the key. 'Chimes inside make the lock vibrate.'

'And that makes it unlock?'

'Yes.'

'But … how?'

'It wants to unlock, so it does.'

Annie really needed something to drink that was stronger than tea. She looked around the room at all the half finished toys, a sudden realisation dawning. 'Did you design that key?'

Isabella nodded. 'Yes.'

'Did you design everything they make at the toy factory?'

Isabella lifted the key and waved it through the air like a child playing with a toy aeroplane.

'Yes,' she said.

17

DISCOVERY

'So, Mrs. Growell is a master chef,' Annie said to Mr. Fairbrother, who was sitting across the table at breakfast, reading the newspaper. 'And Isabella is a creative genius. I'm guessing you can fix anything.'

He shrugged, then gave a sheepish smile. 'Pretty much. Have a little trouble with plumbing but wires and all that, no problem.'

'Is everyone around here a total genius at what they do?'

Mr. Fairbrother nodded. 'Lord Wilf liked excellence.'

'I can gather. I'm starting to feel a little inadequate.'

Mr. Fairbrother grinned. 'Ah, Mistress Annie, you just haven't figured out what it is that you do best yet. I could hazard a guess, having seen all the smiles around the village yesterday, however.'

'What?'

'Making people happy. For all of his creativity and all that, Lord Wilf was a miserable old so-and-so. Never happy about anything. What with her in the kitchen, I sometimes felt in the middle of a glum sandwich.'

Annie couldn't help but smile. 'Well, I appreciate you saying so. I don't really know what else to do. I feel like I'm living in a weird dream.'

'Think it's bad now, give it twenty years. So, what's on today?'

Annie lifted up the key Dave had given her. 'I'm going to have a poke around my grandfather's rooms and see if I can make more sense of things. Then, at eleven o'clock I've got to be at the embarkation ceremony for the steam train. It's been given official approval to start running again, and the first group of tourists should arrive in the afternoon.'

Mr. Fairbrother nodded, then folded over his paper and held it up. 'You made the paper, you notice that? Here, see.'

He passed the paper across the table and Annie's eyes widened at the headline:

Lake District Christmas village finally opens after decades of secrecy

More than twenty years after its conception, Undercastle, the brainchild of reclusive Wilfred Collins of Stone Spire Hall has been given the green light to finally open.

The first tourists are expected to arrive this week. The village, entirely built on private land, is allegedly home to more than a dozen Michelin-starred chefs and bakers, as well as several nationally renowned engineers, tailors, and designers, yet has been in a state of stasis for more than two decades due to its designer's notorious perfectionism.

However, in a surprise move in the wake of Mr. Collins recent death, his heir, Annie Collins of Exeter, Devon has taken the unprecedented step of opening the village to the general public. A local man was quoted as saying, 'About time. Been waiting for that fudge shop to open half my life.'

Annie looked up. 'How did they know all this?'

Mr. Fairbrother gave a sheepish shrug. 'Ah, a few lads pulled up in a Range Rover yesterday. Got stuck on the grid by the main road up there, so I gave them a tug with the tractor.'

'A few … lads?'

Mr. Fairbrother shrugged again. 'Journalists, you know the type.'

'And did you happen to talk to them?'

'Ah, we passed the day a while. Shared a few thoughts on the weather.'

'Well, next time journalists come calling, please let me know.'

'Sure thing, Mistress.'

Annie was just about to say something else, when she caught a glimpse of her own reflection in a mirror on the opposite wall. Who on earth was she starting to sound like, acting all airs and graces with Mr. Fairbrother? She might be sitting on a throne in the middle of the Lake District, but a week before she'd been sitting on a hard, uncomfortable chair in a bank.

'Les, I'm sorry. I didn't mean to sound all snappy.'

'Quite all right, Mistress.'

'No, I really am sorry. I must sound like I've got a pole up my back end.'

Mr. Fairbrother chuckled. 'Well, if you have, you'll have to ask her in the kitchens to fix it. I told you, I'm useless with plumbing.'

Ten minutes later, having cleared her own plates away despite Mrs. Growell's protests, Annie found herself standing outside the door to her grandfather's suite, in her hand the supposedly magic key designed by Isabella.

The lock was tiny but secure, the key large and clunky in her hands. Annie felt like an idiot as she held the key against the lock and tapped it twice against the metal.

Nothing appeared to happen as she stared at the door. She glanced up and down the corridor, afraid someone might have seen her, but the corridor was empty. Lifting the key again, she pressed it to her lips.

'All right,' she whispered. 'Don't fail me this time. You get one last chance, then I'm calling in the demolition squad.'

She tapped the key against the lock again, a little harder this time—

And heard a soft *click* from inside the lock.

Her hand shook as she took hold of the door handle and twisted it, gently opening the door.

Nervous about what she might find inside, she closed her eyes. When she opened them, however, she found that the room was in darkness, all the curtains closed, the light from the corridor extending only a few steps inside, illuminating nothing but a thick grey-blue pile carpet.

She reached a hand up inside the door and found a light switch.

'Okay, revelation, here we come....'

She pressed the switch, and the room appeared before her in a swathe of pale light.

'Huh?'

The curtains were closed, but instead of the clutter Annie had expected, the suite was tidy and well maintained. A large bed was made. A wardrobe stood closed, a single sweater draped over a chair. A coffee mug stood on a desk beside the window, beside it a copy of a newspaper. Annie walked over and found the date to be September the fifth, the day her grandfather had allegedly died.

Annie went to the window and pulled open the curtains, immediately wincing at the sudden brightness. The room looked much better now, with its lingering gloom vanquished. It was rather pleasant in fact, and with views over the forest to the rooftops of Undercastle, backed by snowcapped fells in the distance, Annie felt the inspiration that perhaps her grandfather had once felt when he had embarked on his creative mission. What had led him to keep it all a secret, however, she still didn't know.

Other doors led off from the bedroom. One was an ornate bathroom, another a little kitchen, although the only things Annie found in the cupboards were a couple of packets of coffee and some tins of baked beans, perhaps to keep her grandfather alive during one of the arguments between himself and Mrs. Growell that Mr. Fairbrother had mentioned.

Another door was locked, so Annie pulled out the key and gave the lock a sharp tap. It clicked immediately, and the door swung open. To Annie's surprise, a tinkle of Christmas music began to play, coming from a speaker set into the doorframe itself.

The door opened into what was little more than a closet. A desk dominated the room, but what wall space was left was filled with bookshelves and cabinets. Annie pulled a book off the shelf at random and turned it over to read the title. *Magic and its Truth: Possibilities of Real Magic Existence.* Lifting an eyebrow, she put the book back and took another: *Magic is Real: A Practical Guide to Bringing Magic to Life.* Yet another was called *Modern Day Wizards: Why the World Denies their Existence.*

Her grandfather's obsession was obvious.

He believed in magic.

And not just the kind that people watched on television or attempted to use to impress their friends at parties, but actual, real, bona fide magic.

Annie pulled out the chair and sat down. The seat had the feel of thousands of hours of use, and from the scratches on the desktop edge and the worn circle on the floor where the chair's wheels would have turned, it appeared her grandfather had spent much of his time in wistful contemplation, perhaps reading, perhaps studying.

Annie spun in a slow circle, taking in the tiny room. More lines of shelves contained books on Christmas and its traditions and history. Other shelves had boxes of seemingly random trinkets, which when she rifled through one appeared to be items of magic. Candles. Jars of spices and incense. Wood and metal burners. Yet more candles. Several ornate sticks which looked like the kind of ornamental magic wands you could buy from the back of Sunday newspaper magazines. Annie smiled when she picked up a small round cauldron that had a faint smell of corn soup, and again when she spotted a traditional witches' besom standing in a corner, dust mites caught among its twigs.

A large lower drawer was locked, but again the key opened it. Annie stared at a stack of spiral-wound notebooks, their pages dogeared. The one on the top of the pile was dated from last April. Annie lifted it out and turned to the last page:

September 5ᵗʰ

I'm pretty sure I've got it. Just one more drop of ginseng, ha! Sure I felt a little tingle after all. Definitely it. The residents will be delighted once I allow Mr. Fairbrother to spread the news. Perhaps we can open this year after all. I'll have another try after lunch.

Annie stared at the last thing her grandfather had written, feeling a sense of sadness overcome her. His words, so full of joy, practically jumped off the page. On paper he sounded nothing like the moody old so-and-so Mr. Fairbrother had described.

She closed the book and lifted a stack of the other books below it. They went back years. Her grandfather's life, on paper, right in front of her.

It didn't seem real. She had to pick up several of the notebooks and flip through them, just to make sure they were.

She opened one on a page dated January 10ᵗʰ, 2001.

Our Christmas gift continues to bring joy into our lives. I didn't believe that such happiness could exist again after what happened with my own son, but little Isabella continues to enchant us all. I feel like I've been given a second chance. By night Mrs. Growell nurses her and puts her to bed, and seems like a natural, but by day the girl is mine to entertain. She loves anything that sparkles or tinkles, as is to be expected of her kind.
This morning, with Mr. Fairbrother's help, I strapped her into a carrier on my back, and we went walking in the forest, searching for her family. However, we found no one, and it shames me a little to write it, but I felt glad. They left her for us, and I don't want to give her back.

Annie could only frown as she read the passage over again, worried that she might have misread the implied meaning. Surely her grandfather hadn't believed what she thought he had? That Isabella was an … no. It was ridiculous.

With a funny thought coming to mind, she put the notebook down and picked up one of the books on magic instead. Turning to the copyright page of one, she found it hadn't even been published until after Isabella had arrived.

Her grandfather hadn't surely believed—

A loud rap on the door made Annie jump, almost dropping the book. She put it down and went out of the little study. Another knock came on the suite's entrance door, and when Annie opened it, she found Mr. Fairbrother standing outside, his cheeks flushed as though he had just run up the stairs.

'Ah, Mistress Annie, there you are. I just had a call from the village. They's wondering if you're coming to the opening of the train line or not.'

18

OPENING CEREMONY

ANNIE HAD COMPLETELY LOST TIME IN HER grandfather's suite, and there was no way she would make it to Undercastle in time. When she came out of the front entrance, however, all prepared to have to run the whole way, she found two reindeer outside, harnessed to a quaint, two-man sleigh. Mr. Fairbrother, who had needed to hurry to keep up with her, smiled when she turned to face him.

'You've got to arrive in style,' he said with a smile. 'Can't have you walking there, can we? Plus, been looking forward to getting the old girl back out.'

'The reindeer?'

Mr. Fairbrother chuckled. 'The sleigh. This one's Eileen. They all have names.'

'How many do you have?'

'Five small ones for mucking about in, couple of middle-sized ones for general getting around, and then the big one.'

'The big one?'

'You know, for Christmas.'

Annie gave a slow nod. 'Right.'

'They're all in the garage round the back. I'll show you later. We'd better get moving though. Come on, jump on.'

The reindeer stamped and snorted. One of them twisted its head and appeared to glare at Annie as she inched towards the sleigh.

'Be nice, please,' she whispered, climbing on and sitting down.

'Belt there,' Mr. Fairbrother said. 'Better strap in. These little things don't weigh much and tend to bounce around.' He chuckled. 'Few potholes in the drive, see.'

Annie pulled a seatbelt across herself and clipped it in as Mr. Fairbrother sat down beside her and took hold of the reins. She gave a brief smile as she wondered what her cousin Maggie would think of her now, sitting in a sleigh about to be pulled by a pair of reindeer, then glanced back at the house as though pining for its comforts, and saw Mrs. Growell standing in the entrance, arms folded stiffly across her chest. A moment later, another shape appeared out of the shadows beside her: Isabella. With a wide grin, Isabella lifted a hand to wave.

'Reet,' Mr. Fairbrother said, snapping the reins. 'Come on, Eileen.'

The two reindeer leapt forward. Mr. Fairbrother let out a delighted chortle as he nearly rolled backwards out of the seat, his legs flying up in front of him.

'You should put your seatbelt on,' Annie gasped, holding on to a side bar with all her strength.

'Ha,' Mr. Fairbrother gasped. 'Where would be the fun in that?'

The sleigh bumped and jerked over the snowy ground as the reindeer bustled off towards the trees. Mr. Fairbrother acted like a kid at an amusement park, leaning out of the side as they went round corners, theatrically jumping out of his seat with each bump.

'That's it,' he said, as they crested a rise along the forest path and then accelerated quickly down the slope on the other side. Instead of feeling sick as she had expected, however, Annie realised she was having fun. Her heart was thundering, but instead of screaming at each bump and jerk, she found herself laughing.

'Woo!' she cried as they sped around a corner, the sleigh leaning so far she thought they might topple out. 'Come on, ah … what are their names? Kevin and Roland?'

Mr. Fairbrother laughed. 'Nae, this pair are lassies, aren't they? Otherwise they'd have lost their antlers for winter. These two ladies are Glitter and Tinkerbell.' At Annie's frown, he added, 'Isabella named them.'

A small crowd had gathered on the station platform. The train, a beautiful ornate steam train rather strangely named Mr. Johnson according to the red sign along its black locomotive, puffed steam into the air in readiness. As Annie, led by Mr. Fairbrother, climbed up on to the platform, she recognised most of the people she had got to know over the last few days. There was Dave from the Wonder Toy Studios, dressed in full elf regalia, Reg the greengrocer, Diane and Frank from the pancake house and fudge shops respectively. And there, standing at the back … were Mrs. Growell and Isabella.

'How on earth did they get here before us?' Annie whispered to Mr. Fairbrother.

'Ah, took the Range Rover, didn't they?'

'The … Range Rover.' Annie sighed. 'Perhaps you can point it out to me sometime.'

Mr. Fairbrother grinned. 'Ah, but the sleigh was more fun, hey?'

Annie had to admit that he was right, but there was no time left for discussion as a tall, rotund man in a top hat stepped forward.

'Hey Bill,' Annie said, remembering the station master from the village meeting.

'You have to call me Willy Whistle today,' Bill said, winking as he doffed his hat to her. Then, in a louder voice, he turned to the crowd and called, 'Everyone, thank you for coming! Today is a day that we've been long expecting. Now, without further ado, I'd like to welcome our esteemed patron, Miss Annie Collins of Stone Spire Hall to cut the tape, and on this date, December the first, officially declare Undercastle open for business.'

The crowd cheered. Bill waved Annie forward and led her to a podium by the head of the train. A thick ticker tape in red and green stripes hung across from the station building to the locomotive's funnel, dipping in the middle to be within Annie's reach. As she stood on the podium, Annie reached down and literally pinched herself.

'I'm a bank clerk,' she muttered under her breath, before hearing her voice amplifying around her and realising that a microphone on top of a dais was already switched on. As a few people chuckled, Annie gave a sheepish grin and cleared her throat.

'Ah … hello,' she said, clenching a fist by her side and attempting to channel her inner politician. Had it not been so cold she would surely have been visibly sweating, and as it was her blouse had stuck itself to her back and refused to let go.

'My name is Annie … Collins, and … it's … ah … lovely to have … the … ah … honour of saying….' She trailed off, glancing up above the crowd, remembering how a teacher had once told her that if you got nervous while making a speech you should avoid looking directly at anyone but instead look over the top of their heads. And there, across the street, she saw a line of Christmas lights glittering in the upstairs window of a cottage. Lifting one hand, she grinned. 'Merry Christmas, everyone!'

The crowd began to applaud. Annie, feeling a fresh surge of confidence, leaned closer to the microphone and said, 'I've only been here a short time, but the welcome I've received has warmed my heart, and I'm sure you'll all extend the same welcome to all the people who are going to come here. I mean, the visitors. Great job, everyone.'

She lifted a hand and made a fist. People started to clap again.

'You have to cut the tape and declare the train line open,' Bill hissed from beside her.

'Ah, right. Okay, we're open!' Annie shouted, then picked up the shears and cut the tape to cheers and more applause. Bill waved a hand, and somewhere behind the station a couple of fireworks exploded into the sky, before the train gave a sharp whistle. Annie looked out across the crowd and saw Isabella jump up and down before grabbing Mrs. Growell around the shoulders, shaking the statue-stiff woman like a shop's mannequin. Mr. Fairbrother gave her a thumbs' up, then turned to shake hands with a man dressed rather randomly as a circus clown. Annie watched the train chugging out of the station, gently arcing along the line until it disappeared around the curve of the valley, until only a column of steam was visible rising out of the pine tree forest.

'Nice speech.'

Annie turned. Diane Jenkins was standing beside the dais, a wide smile on her face.

'Ah, thanks. I'm afraid I'm not good at these things.'

'You did great. The whole village is buzzing now. Are you coming to the after party?'

'What after party?'

'At Frank's place. Although I'm supplying pancakes, and Harriet from the Hot Chocolate Emporium will be on drinks duty. The first village party of the season, and likely the first of many. And you're the guest of honour.'

Annie could only stare. 'Ah, thanks.'

'So I'll see you there?'

Annie nodded, then peered through the crowd, looking for Mrs. Growell, Isabella, and Mr. Fairbrother. She spotted them near the edge of the platform. Mr. Fairbrother was talking to Dave, who was gesturing wildly as though describing a fight with a bear. Mrs. Growell stood beside him with her arms folded, Isabella beside her, holding on to Mrs. Growell's elbow. There was something about them both—

'I just need to speak to my ... uh, staff,' Annie said. 'You know, just to make sure they weren't planning to sneak off.'

Diane grinned. 'You're the lady of the hall now,' she said.

'I know,' Annie said as she watched Mrs. Growell, Isabella, and Mr. Fairbrother, feeling more awkward than ever.

PART II

THE STRANGER

19

A STRANGER ARRIVES

'So you'll be here on the seventeenth?'

'Most definitely. Darren got the time off work and we'll have the car ready to go as soon as the kids get home from school. I'm keeping it as a surprise.'

'They'll love it here. I mean, it was a bit weird when I first showed up, but now that the village is filled with people, it's just magical. I've never seen anything like it. Yesterday we had a ceremony to officially "open" the Christmas tree, this massive pine they have in the village square. I've never seen so much hot chocolate, and people were dancing around it until midnight. My thighs were killing me this morning.'

'Got to burn off those calories somehow.'

Annie nodded, barely able to believe her own words. 'I'm going ice-skating this morning. There's a kind of shallow inlet on the lake which they cordon off so that it can completely freeze over. It's just … magical. Have I said that already?'

'Sounds amazing. So, you're not coming back then?'

Annie's cheeks flushed. She'd made a phone call that

morning and asked for another week off work. She'd planned to hand in her notice, but her gut had prevented her. She couldn't quite bring herself to pull the plug completely, when everything was still so weird. Even though she was getting used to Stone Spire Hall and Undercastle, she still didn't feel like she belonged here. And her grandfather's notes and letters, when she had time to go through them, were only making things stranger.

'Not for the time being. I'm undecided, to be honest. I mean, I like it here and everything, but, you know, it's kind of weird.'

'Like a lottery win? You know, I know a guy who won fifty grand on a scratch card and just stuffed it in the charity box at Tesco. Said it was all about the thrill of the chase, but it kind of took the meaning out of everything when he actually won it.'

Annie chuckled. 'That's exactly how it feels. I mean, I don't deserve any of this. I've never done anything special. It's just too … weird.'

'Don't beat yourself up about it. Troy was a turkey, the way he treated you. You earned a bit of good karma.'

Annie shrugged. 'A bit, maybe, but not an entire lorry load.'

'Well, don't turn your nose up at it. And you never know, Troy might just turn up and ruin it.'

Annie felt a shiver of dread. 'I hope not.'

'Just play it by ear, eh.'

'Will do. See you on the seventeenth?'

'Absolutely. Get the hot chocolates and the fudge ready.' Julie chuckled. 'I'm thinking of starving the kids for a couple of days just so they hit the ground running.'

'I'll tell the man who runs the fudge shop to double down.'

'Good plan. Right. I'd better get these guys off to school.'

Annie said goodbye to Julie and hung up. Outside the window, a light snow was falling, the ground already carpeted with a gentle blanket of white. Annie put her phone down on the windowsill—she'd found her Grandfather's suite to be the only place in the house with decent reception—and went back into his study. There was still half an hour until the breakfast bell would ring, and Annie still had stacks of her grandfather's old notebooks to read through.

Life in the hall was busy, and as the Lady in Residence —as people kept calling her, despite her insistence not to— there were constant demands on her time. She enjoyed it for the most part, but there was only so much fudge and so many pancakes she could eat, and if she drank any more hot chocolate she'd sprout roots and turn into a cacao tree. As a result, she'd not had nearly the amount of time she would have liked to figure out everything that had inadvertently brought her here.

Glancing up at the clock, she sat down, first picking up the notebooks on the desk which she'd marked with post-it notes.

I tried to call Richard again today. I asked him if he'd consider moving up here and bringing Annie. I think that's the missing ingredient: a little bit of wide-eyed wonder. Only a child really believes. She'd be able to see it, I'm sure. And then I'd know that everything I've worked for all this time was worth it. Of course he said no. And then he said to stop calling. I have to say, it cut like a knife. He was always such a practical boy. I wish he'd open his eyes a little wider sometimes. He's missing out on so much.

The gentle estrangement between her grandfather and

her father was often alluded to, and Annie felt a sense of regret that they hadn't solved their differences before her father's unexpected death. From reading her grandfather's notes, it seemed there had been no big argument, just a gradual parting, a diversion of their lives. Her father had done his best for his family, and her grandfather, as he became more introverted and reclusive, had gradually been cut out of their lives.

However, the appearance of Isabella had done nothing but fill her grandfather with a sense of wonder.

I'd swear they're out there at night, listening and watching, checking up on her. I see their lights sometimes, out in the woods, but I think they know she's safe. Her laughter echoes through the halls, bringing joy to every corner of this place, and I can feel the magic in her whenever she smiles. She was our gift from them, and I know to the bottom of my heart that Isabella was my second chance.

His notes talked often of lights in the woods, of supposed fairies and elves. Annie, brought up on her dad's practicality, was aware such things were a load of rubbish. Part of her thought that her grandfather's insistence that they were real was sweet, another part that it was weird. From what she'd heard from the residents of Undercastle, her grandfather had been kind and gentle, but also slightly off his rocker.

She was just about to open another notebook when the bell rang, calling her for breakfast.

Downstairs, Mr. Fairbrother was in position with his paper over his knees as usual, a bacon and egg sandwich and a coffee on a tray in front of him. To Annie's surprise, for the first time the fourth place was laid up for breakfast, and as she sat down, she heard voices on the stairs to the kitchens.

'There's no need to skip up the stairs, dear. You might drop something.'

Mrs. Growell, as stern as ever, came into view. Behind her came Isabella, carrying a tray in one hand and a teapot by the handle in the other. She appeared to be playing a game of hopscotch up the stairs, while somehow avoiding spilling anything. As they reached the table, Isabella gave Annie a wide grin.

'Good morning, Mistress … Annie,' Mrs. Growell said, then set down a bowl in front of Annie, followed by a small jug of milk. 'As requested … Coco Pops.'

Annie grinned. 'Fantastic.'

Mrs. Growell gave Annie a stony-faced stare. 'May I politely request that you endeavour to challenge my culinary skills a little more in future?'

'I'd be delighted to see how they tasted homemade….'

'Such a trivial breakfast. With so many options may I ask of what is the appeal of something so simplistic?'

'Dad wouldn't let us have anything with a high sugar content,' Annie said, as Isabella, also sporting a bowl of Coco Pops, along with a chopped apple and a bowl of yoghurt, sat down beside her, grinning wildly like a child at a birthday party. She leaned against Annie and gave her shoulder a nudge before chuckling quietly to herself.

'Appropriate,' Mrs. Growell said tersely. 'It sounds like your father was a firm and well ordered man.'

'No doubt why he fell out with the master,' Mr. Fairbrother quipped, then quickly buried his head behind his newspaper as Mrs. Growell's fearsome eyes turned on him.

'Dad was pretty strict about what we ate,' Annie said. 'Although as a result I have nearly perfect teeth.' She gave

Mrs. Growell a wide grin, winning a giggle from Isabella. 'However, I did attempt to destroy them with ice-cream during my divorce.'

Mrs. Growell had no smile to drop, but she gave a thoughtful nod. 'Unfortunate,' she said, before lowering herself neatly into her seat, throwing Isabella a stern, motherly glance as the girl rocked back on her chair, before nearly falling off and having to grab Mr. Fairbrother's arm to steady herself.

'That looks nice,' Annie said, peering across the table at Mrs. Growell's single slice of toast, a nub of butter gradually melting in the exact centre.

Mrs. Growell gave a tense nod, then picked up her knife and began to spread the butter in gentle, rhythmic strokes. Mr. Fairbrother took it upon himself to pour tea into cups, while Isabella catapulted a stray Coco Pop from her tray into Annie's bowl with a flick of her knife, giving Annie a shy grin. The scowl from Mrs. Growell wasn't quite as harsh as Annie might have received, but Isabella's smile momentarily dropped, before returning as soon as Mrs. Growell looked away.

'What's on today's schedule?' Mr. Fairbrother asked, putting his paper down and taking a sip of tea. 'Looks like the snow's in for the day, so I'll be busy clearing that path I imagine.'

'I planned to give the kitchen floor a deep clean,' Mrs. Growell said.

As usual, Isabella said nothing, but watched Annie with a twinkle of amusement in her eyes.

Annie couldn't help but smile. 'There's an, um, fudge pie competition this afternoon that I've been asked to, er, judge.'

Mr. Fairbrother chuckled. 'A what?'

'The contestants get an hour to make the most creative

pie using only fudge and other confectionary,' Annie said. 'The winner will get the inaugural Fudge Pie Trophy, and then the entries will get auctioned off, with the money going to charity.'

'Ha!' Isabella cried, clapping her hands together.

'Manners, dear,' Mrs. Growell said, giving the girl a stern look.

'What happens to all the, um, trimmings and stuff?' Mr. Fairbrother said with a sheepish glance.

Annie grimaced. 'The judges—who are basically me, Frank and Diane—are required to clean up.'

'Well, bring me back a doggy bag,' Mr. Fairbrother said with a wink. 'Me and Marge'll go halves down in the kitchen.'

'I will not lower myself to eat table scraps from some fudge competition,' Mrs. Growell snapped, even as Isabella grinned and patted her on the shoulder.

'Ah, come on,' Mr. Fairbrother said. 'Might sweeten you up a bit.'

The fudge pie competition proved as interesting and stomach-filling as Annie had expected, but barely was she able to sit down before she was required to attend the first banquet dinner of the year at the village's only hotel, Winter Sky Lodge. Having forgotten to tell Mrs. Growell she would be out for dinner, she made a quick phone call to the house, where she received a stern, 'I would appreciate advance notice in future,' for her troubles. Feeling a little guilty, she nevertheless enjoyed the meal, up until she was asked rather abruptly to make a speech to the assembled customers. Having drank too much wine, she bumbled her way through it, finishing with a hearty,

'Merry Christmas!' which brought cheers and raised glasses.

Afterwards, she felt too excited to go straight back to the hall, even though Mr. Fairbrother had promised to come out and pick her up any time she called. With a light snow falling and Undercastle glittering with Christmas lights, the cobblestone streets and stonewalled houses took on a magical, otherworldly quality. Annie wandered from one end of the village to the other, marvelling at the Christmas trees shining from inside lattice windows, listening to the tinkle of Christmas music. She sighed at the sight of a young couple sitting on a bench in the snow, their heads leaning against each other, their hands entwined. She smiled at a couple of children—who probably should have been in bed by now—chasing each other through the snow while their mothers called for order. Christmas had come, and with it her life and fortunes had overturned. She had fallen down an abyss and emerged into a magical world, somehow landing on her feet.

She headed back through the village, planning to use the payphone in the station, because one of Undercastle's quirks was to have no cellular connection. In her grandfather's notebooks Annie had found a paragraph complaining about the invasion of mobile phones to every part of life, and how he had hoped Undercastle might have been free from such a plague. While it made life a fraction more awkward than Annie would have liked, nevertheless a late night visit to the pretty train station, illuminated with Christmas light and glittering under a blanket of snow, was of no great concern. During the day Bill kept a vat of hot chocolate warm over a stove ready to greet the incoming passengers, and there was likely some left over.

Gentle background music greeted her as she climbed

the steps on to the platform. The snow had fallen over the tracks but left most of the platform free. Christmas lights were strung along the edge of the overhanging roof, fed through the wrought iron decorative fixtures, lending the platform a calm and warmth that defied the falling snow and the chill in the air. The train had recently departed for its final evening trip to Penrith, taking the last group of day trippers home.

The payphone was at the platform's far end. Annie walked along the tiles, her hands in her pockets, humming to herself. The payphone was just up ahead, but as she passed the final pillar before reaching it, she let out a little gasp.

A man was lying on a bench next to the wall, a small bag tucked under his head and a thick duffel coat draped over him.

Annie was about to go back to the station office to call whoever was on duty when the man shifted, turning over. He looked to be about forty, and wasn't the ragamuffin she had initially expected. He wore nice shoes—if inappropriate for winter—and his hair was neatly cut. He had a kind, peaceful face, and looked like a teacher or a social worker. Annie found herself leaning over him, frowning, as he suddenly opened his eyes.

Annie gasped again and jumped back as the man sat up. She retreated a few steps, nearly slipped off the platform edge, and only recovered with an awkward, embarrassing flail of the arms. As she stumbled forwards again, narrowly avoiding the pillar, the man twisted around on the seat and pulled the coat over his shoulders.

'I'm sorry to have startled you,' he said. 'I'm afraid I missed the last train, and had nowhere else to sleep. I … couldn't afford to stay at the hotel, but I imagine it's fully booked anyway.'

As he adjusted his clothing, Annie noticed a patch on the elbow of his sweater, and a tear on the lining of his coat that had been sewn up with awkward, unskilled stitches. She almost smiled; she'd had to do the same to a couple of her own jackets. Unable to help herself, she glanced at his hands, looking for any sign of a ring, but to her disappointment he was wearing gloves.

'You shouldn't stay out here,' she said. 'It'll get much colder yet.'

The man smiled and patted a stomach that looked lean beneath his sweater. 'Don't worry, I have plenty of winter protection.'

Annie doubted it from the narrow angles of his face. 'I'll call the station master. At least you could sit inside.'

'It's all right. The first departure is at six, and it's what … eleven now?'

Annie glanced up at the clock on the station wall. 'Twenty past. You can't stay out here for the next seven hours. You'll freeze.'

The man smiled again. 'It's okay. I really don't mind.'

Annie watched him, then realised he was doing the same to her, and quickly looked away. *How much wine did I drink?*

'Sorry,' she muttered. 'I didn't mean to stare. I drank a bit too much and you're blurring a little bit.'

'I'm the one in the middle,' he said.

'Did you just come for a day trip?' Annie asked, then internally scolded herself for hunting ways to continue their conversation when she should be getting the man out of the cold. 'Sorry, look, come with me. There'll be a heater on inside. I don't think the station master will mind us sitting in the waiting room.' *Us? What am I thinking?*

'Well, if you insist, but I don't mind.'

Annie forced herself to turn away, and led the stranger

back along the platform. She knew he was following from the soft tap of his shoes on the tiles. The waiting room was halfway along, but the light was off. Annie went inside and switched on the light, then turned on the heater in the corner. As the man came in and sat down on a bench by the wall, he rubbed his hands together.

'It'll warm up in a minute,' Annie said.

'Sorry, I didn't realise this room was open,' said the man. Then, with a smile, he added, 'To answer your question, I'm not really sure how long I was coming for. I just needed to see the place, to pay my respects. Are you staying here, or are you working?'

'I'm … ah, both really,' Annie said, intrigued by his choice of words. 'I'm kind of working here, and staying at the same time.'

'In one of the shops?'

Annie shrugged. 'Uh, general maintenance, I suppose you'd say.'

'Well, it's a beautiful place.' He gave a little sigh. 'I can see why people might want to stay. Sorry, my name's Ray. Raymond Burns.' He gave a little chuckle. 'Say it fast.'

'Ray … oh.'

Ray smiled. 'Yeah. My school friends loved it. But, you know, kids are kids. Lad in my class was called William Tinkerbottom, so he took most of what I might have got otherwise.'

'I see. Ah, my name's Annie.'

Ray put out a hand. 'Well, it's nice to meet you Annie, on this cold, dark night.'

She took his hand. His palm was cold but soft, his fingers gentle. He ducked his head in a little bow as he squeezed her hand, then let go.

'You make yourself comfortable, and I'll go and see if there's anything to drink in the station building,' Annie said. 'I know the station master usually makes a pot of hot chocolate during the day.'

'Sure, thanks. That would be nice.'

Annie smiled, then turned and went through a door to the station concourse. The station master's room was a little further along, and after explaining to the man on night duty what she wanted, she was able to make a couple of cups of hot chocolate from what had been left over during the day. Worried that Ray might not have eaten, she popped a couple of marshmallows on the side of the saucer, then headed back to the waiting room.

Ray … it was an old-fashioned name that was now back in vogue, as name cycles turned, she thought. Not so dissimilar to her own name really. Ray Burns … it was a little cringeworthy but Raymond was fine. She wondered who he was. He seemed friendly, had a nice smile.

Annie … what's going on?

She stopped by the door to the waiting room, wondering if she ought to plan what she was going to say.

Don't be ridiculous. He's just a guy I met on a station platform.

In the aftermath of her divorce from Troy, Julie had suggested all manner of options to get Annie's love life back on track, from singles apps to bizarre speed dating events, but the emotional fallout had left Annie too scared to consider anything. And surviving the sheer poverty that the divorce settlement had plunged her into had taken up whatever energy was left. Troy had set out to rip out her soul, and had managed it rather well, leaving Annie like a smoking bomb crater. However, the unforeseen circumstances that had brought her to this train station in the middle of nowhere had gone some way to refilling the crater of her life and had even planted a few flowers. Perhaps it was time.

And after all, it doesn't look like he's with anyone. Otherwise, what would he be doing here on his own?

Finally deciding to at least try to keep the conversation going a little longer, Annie steeled herself and pushed through the doors.

At the sight of Ray, she stopped.

He lay stretched out on one of the benches, his jacket pulled over him like a blanket, his eyes closed, a gentle smile on his face.

Annie let out a sigh. He looked so peaceful, so she couldn't wake him. After a moment's thought, she set down the hot chocolate near his head, but just far enough away that he wouldn't knock it if he woke suddenly. Then, as an afterthought, she put her own marshmallows alongside his. He probably needed the energy.

Then, giving the sleeping man a brief, regretful smile, she switched off the light and went out, taking her own cup back to the station master's office, before hurrying off to call Mr. Fairbrother.

After all, it was getting late.

20

MAGIC IN THE SNOW

I do feel bad about what I said. I didn't mean it, but it looks like I might have driven a real wedge between Richard and myself. He's a good boy, if unimaginative, but I didn't need to tell him so. And claiming he couldn't really be my son ... well, that was foolhardy. I'm sure I'll get a chance to make it up to him.

THE WORDS IN ISOLATION MIGHT NOT HAVE MEANT much, but the date did. One week before her father's unexpected death. He had gone on a business trip, and had been driving uncharacteristically fast along a narrow stretch of road. A tractor pulling out of a field gateway had had no chance to get out of his way. Her father's car had flipped and ended up in the field.

She had been searching for something specific in her grandfather's diaries that might give some idea to what had happened between her grandfather and her father, and while she thought she might have found it, she really wanted to talk to her mother. However, with her mother off on an adventure holiday, she was stuck.

Instead, she wandered around the house with her head

hung low, brooding until Mrs. Growell snapped at her to stop wearing out the carpet and do something useful. Isabella had left her gloves at the house yesterday, and would Annie mind walking up to Isabella's cottage to return them?

It was a strange request that only made Annie wonder more about something she had been considering since first seeing the two of them together, but as she needed an excuse to get out of the house, she agreed.

Once she was outside, trudging through several inches of snow, she immediately felt better. The fresh air, the clear blue sky, the tinkle of Christmas music that never seemed far away … it all made her feel refreshed and blew her problems away like the seeds of a dandelion caught on a summer breeze.

As she caught sight of a few of the reindeer nosing through the snow, she realised that she was even beginning to warm to them. It might be a while before she could refer to them by their supposed given names, but maybe in time….

The forest felt pristine and untouched. The trees creaked and groaned, the smell of pine cones filled her nostrils, and she began to sense some of the magic her grandfather had believed in. Everything was so peaceful, a million miles from having crazy guys trying to climb over partition screens.

Isabella had been absent from breakfast this morning, her absence explained by Mr. Fairbrother with a shrug and Mrs. Growell a frustrated sigh. Now, on the path up to her hidden cottage, there were no tracks to indicate the girl had been outside this morning, only light depressions covered in fresh snow. Lights shone in her cottage windows, however, and before Annie could even reach the gate, the front door opened and Isabella stepped out, wearing a thick jacket, fake fur framing her face. She looked more elfish than ever, lacking only the green tights and pointy shoes. At the sight of Annie she gave a wide smile and lifted her hand to wave.

'You left your gloves in the house,' Annie said, sticking a hand into her jacket pocket and pulling out a pair of insulated winter mittens that looked hand-stitched.

'Ah, yes,' Isabella said, giving a frantic nod. 'I know.'

Annie got the impression that Isabella had left the gloves behind on purpose, and that she had known Mrs. Growell might ask Annie to return them. While such an idea seemed farfetched, Annie was beginning to realise that life at Stone Spire Hall didn't follow conventional norms. So when Isabella held up a bag and pointed at a path that led up past her house into the forest, Annie just smiled and nodded.

There wasn't much in the way of conversation as they walked deeper into the trees, before the path began to wind gradually uphill. Annie tried asking a few questions to which Isabella answered with one to three words each, sometimes only with a nod or a little chuckle. Soon, however, the path got too steep for easy conversation, and Annie found herself out of breath as they trudged upwards through the snow.

Twenty minutes of arduous hiking later, however, they emerged from the forest onto a grassy hilltop. The path led away northwards, sloping gently down into snow-covered moorland, but from the hill's crest a panoramic view of Undercastle, the lake, and the fells on the other side spread out before them. The majesty of everything took away what breath the climb hadn't, and for a few minutes Annie just stood and stared at the view, taking in the rolling fells and the forested valley, feeling so small yet so alive at the same time. Life might be flawed, she thought, but here at least it was beautiful.

Beside her, Isabella was fumbling around inside the bag she had brought. Finally, with a satisfied 'Aha!' she pulled out something made out of wood with a silvery base. It was all pistons and cogs and about the size of a dinner plate. With a smile, she held it out to Annie.

Annie stared. It was a clockwork bird. With so many moving parts it looked fragile, delicate.

Isabella, grinning, pulled something else out of her bag. It was a tube of metal with notches cut into it, about the length of Isabella's forearm. Taking another metal pipe about the size of a paint brush, Isabella tapped the larger pipe, causing a high-pitched ringing sound.

To Annie's shock, the contraption in her hands jerked. She made to drop it, but Isabella gave a frantic shake of her head, then nodded up at the sky.

'Throw,' she said.

'Are you sure?'

'Yes. Watch.'

'All right, then. But I don't want to break it.'

'Don't worry.'

Annie spread her feet and set herself, ready to catch the wooden bird when it came back down. 'Okay … three … two … one—'

She tossed the wooden bird a couple of feet into the air. Expecting its swift return, she reached out for it, but to her delighted surprise its wings opened out like a miniature umbrella, pieces of canvas sewn between the folds of its wooden features. Then, even more amazingly, Isabella began to tap on her metal pole, creating a strange ringing tune. With each resonant note, the bird's wings flapped. It rose slowly above them, holding itself steady in the wind buffeting over the hilltop. Annie glanced at Isabella and saw the girl frowning with deep concentration as she played. Then, as another gust of wind took the bird sideways, her playing became more frantic, discordant. The bird gave a manic, off-balance flap, then crashed to earth.

As Annie picked it up and wiped snow away, Isabella let out a sigh, then grinned. 'Not yet,' she said. She took the bird from Annie, lifted a section of wing where the canvas had ripped, then shrugged. 'Next time.'

Annie stared at her. 'I can't believe what I just saw,' she said. 'You made that thing fly using that instrument, didn't you?'

Isabella shrugged. 'Nearly.' Then, with a giggle, she added, 'One or two adjustments maybe.'

'That was....'

Isabella tucked a strand of hair behind her ear, the little point protruding from beneath her woolly hat. 'Magic?'

'I wouldn't have believed it if I hadn't seen it.'

Isabella shrugged again, then dropped the wooden bird back into the bag. She turned and headed back to the path leading down into the woods, with Annie trailing along behind her. Just before they reached the trail head, however, Annie noticed another figure in the distance, following a different path that headed down from the peak, arcing around the hill to the left, presumably to arrive back in Undercastle. The figure was heading their way. While Annie couldn't see the person's face clearly, she recognised the jacket.

Ray Burns.

So, he was still here. She paused for a moment, then called to Isabella. 'Uh, there's someone over there who I met yesterday. I'm just going to say hello.'

Isabella lifted the bag. 'Fix,' she said, which Annie took to mean they were going their separate ways.

'Okay,' she said.

As Isabella wandered off down into the woods, humming to herself like a joyful Red Riding Hood knowing the wolf was already dead, Annie walked down the path towards Ray, trying to act as though she hadn't seen him. Ray, however, was walking slowly, his head down, as though the climb were far steeper than a gentle slope.

'Hello,' Annie said brightly, when she was both close enough and during a brief respite in the wind.

Ray lifted his head. He looked exhausted, but at the sight of Annie he gave a wide smile. 'Wow, what a surprise,' he said, stumbling closer, slipping a little. 'Are you one for scenery too?'

'I got tricked into some exercise,' Annie said. 'But it's lovely up here, if a little chilly. So … you decided to stay?'

Ray nodded. He shook a lump of snow off one foot, and to Annie's surprise she saw he was wearing the same shoes as yesterday: slightly scuffed office shoes which were wholly inappropriate for hiking in the snow. His shoes, socks, and trousers halfway to his knees were soaked and mud stained.

'I wasn't ready to leave just yet,' Ray said. His eyes met Annie's as he spoke and she felt a little flutter. He had nice eyes, and a kind smile, even if he didn't understand weather-appropriate clothing. 'I decided to stay a little longer.'

'Did you find somewhere to stay?'

Ray gave a momentary frown, then nodded. 'Yes.'

'I'm glad to hear it.'

They both fell silent. Annie realised she was blocking Ray's way to the peak, so she stepped off the path and waited until he started moving again, smiling as he walked past her, then pausing a few steps further along and looking back until she followed. She thought about mentioning the shoes, but Ray didn't seem bothered.

He reached the small peak where Annie had been standing with Isabella just minutes before, pulled off a hat he wore and dropped it down at his feet. Annie frowned. She was just wondering whether to mention it when Ray suddenly cupped his hands around his mouth and hollered, '*Hello?*' at the top of his voice.

As the echo reverberated across the valley, Ray turned to look at Annie and grinned. 'I've always wanted to do that,' he said. 'Why don't you try it?'

Annie winced and shook her head. 'No, it's okay. I, ah, have a bit of a sore throat.'

Ray cocked his head. 'I was thinking of going and getting a large hot chocolate and a cream-stuffed pancake as a reward for making it all the way up here,' he said. 'It might help your throat….'

One voice was screaming at Annie to say yes, but another—the one that remembered the shoes, the dropped hat, and the sudden shout—was calling for a no. While caution didn't quite win, it swayed her enough to make her say, 'Ah, I've got some things to do….'

'It's okay. It was nice to see you again. Thanks for yesterday.'

'No problem.'

'Did you come up the same way? I didn't see any other tracks.'

Annie shook her head. 'No, through the forest.'

Ray nodded. 'That's too bad. Anyway, it was nice to meet you again, Annie.'

The way he said her name gave Annie butterflies in her stomach, but she could only give a dumb grin as Ray reached down and picked up his hat, before heading back down the path the same way he had come.

He was almost out of sight around the curve of the hill before he paused and turned back. Seeing her still standing there, he lifted a hand and waved. Then, as he disappeared out of sight, Annie slapped the side of her leg and let out a sigh.

Why didn't I wave back?

21

THE MYSTERY DEEPENS

Richard told me to stop sending Christmas cards. Honestly, I find his attitude a little distasteful, but it's his choice, and I respect it. He thinks I've lost my mind, but he doesn't understand. No one does. They weren't there.

ANNIE PUT DOWN THE DIARY WITH A SIGH AND REACHED for the cup of coffee beside the desk. The diary, a tattered old thing barely held together by its metal coil, dated from a couple of years prior to her father's death. Her grandfather, from what she had read, had given up on repairing his relationship with her father, but had made occasional forays aimed at contacting her, it seemed. Annie, though, didn't want to read any further, particularly on the cusp of Christmas. These things had happened in the past, and it felt best to leave them there. The more she read, the more she found herself disliking her grandfather, his flippant attitude towards normal life and endless pursuit of the imaginary, all while living the charmed existence of one born into money.

It left a sour taste in her mouth, particularly as she was now doing the same.

Downstairs, she knocked on the kitchen door, then requested a plastic bag and a pair of tongs from Mrs. Growell.

'What do you need those for?' Mrs. Growell asked with a stern glare.

'I'm going to pick up litter,' Annie said. 'I want to do something useful.'

'There isn't any. Mr. Fairbrother leads a group every Sunday morning who go out and do it. You won't find so much as a discarded tissue within a five-mile radius.'

'I have to do something useful.' Annie shook her head and sighed. 'I have to do something to justify my existence. I don't feel like I deserve to be here.'

'Life is a lottery,' Mrs. Growell said. Then, with an uncharacteristic half-smile, she added, 'I have some mince pies I promised to bake for tomorrow's street party. If you have nothing better to do … you could help me.' She gave a little cough. 'Mistress.'

Annie smiled. She remembered hearing Diane mention the party, something that the residents planned to do every Saturday right through December.

'Great,' she said, clapping her hands together loud enough to bring a grimace from Mrs. Growell. 'What do you want me to do?'

Mrs. Growell proved to be a hard, regimented task master, but having taken on the job of preparing three hundred mince pies, there wasn't much room for improvisation, and within a few minutes Annie felt like she was doing real work for the first time in her life, her arms aching as she rolled and pressed pastry, scooped mincemeat, loaded and unloaded an industrial sized oven with trays of mince pies.

'You're good at this,' she told Mrs. Growell, as the housekeeper moved her fingers over a tray of freshly prepared mince pies, pushing and prodding until each pie was near identical.

'My background was in catering,' Mrs. Growell said, 'But I honed my skills in this very kitchen ... despite the décor.'

'Would you like it changed?'

Mrs. Growell almost—but not quite—smiled. 'I would very much like it changed,' she said. 'It has always felt like something of a mockery. I understand what your grandfather intended ... but like many of his plans, it was somewhat misguided.'

It was rare to find Mrs. Growell in such a garrulous mood. 'I'll ask Mr. Fairbrother if he knows any local building firms who could take care of it,' she said, then, before Mrs. Growell could shut up shop again, quickly added, 'You know, I was wondering why there aren't any pictures of Grandfather anywhere. I haven't found a single one. It seems weird to say it, but I have no idea what he looks like.'

Mrs. Growell gave a slow nod. 'Your grandfather didn't appreciate such things,' she said. 'He believed they were dampeners for the imagination.'

'What on earth does that mean?'

Mrs. Growell gave a quiet sigh, and Annie wondered if the housekeeper was upset. Then, as Mrs. Growell actually, genuinely smiled this time, she realised otherwise. Perhaps living under the same roof as her increasingly eccentric grandfather had given her frustrations that were only just starting to bubble to the surface.

'The best way I could explain it is to think of a

childhood memory, one that you remember fondly. A place you visited, a person you knew, a kind grandparent, perhaps. That memory is treasured, sacred. Having a photograph—or worse, a video recording—of that same event can only serve to remove the sprinkling of magic that memory had lent it. Have you heard of the Cottingley Fairies?'

Annie frowned. 'You mean those fake pictures of the cardboard cutout fairies that everyone thought were real?'

Mrs. Growell nodded. 'Your grandfather believed they were real.'

'But even the girls admitted they were fake, didn't they?'

'I believe so, although the details of the story elude me. However, your grandfather thought otherwise. He felt that they had been real in the minds of the children, and would have stayed that way had the photographs never been taken. The experience would have become a treasured memory for those children, one that would have become more magical with the passing of time.'

Annie gave a slow nod. 'Rose-coloured glasses,' she said.

'Wilfred felt that modern society, with its endless recording of every moment, had destroyed the magic in the world, left it empty and soulless. And … he had taken it upon himself to somehow bring the magic back.'

'How?'

'We didn't know. But he felt that here, out in the country where you could breathe the fresh air, there was real magic at play. And if you waited long enough, you would see it.'

'And then he found Isabella.'

Mrs. Growell nodded. 'She was his proof. He believed she had come from the forest.'

'But she hadn't, had she?'

Mrs. Growell gave a slight tilt of the head that wasn't quite a nod, wasn't quite a shake. 'That's not for me to say. Your grandfather believed it.'

They lapsed into silence for a while as they dealt with a couple of freshly baked trays, removing them from the oven, flipping the finished mince pies onto cooling racks, then loading the oven with the next batches. Finally, as the last batch went into the oven, Mrs. Growell said, 'Would you like tea, dear?'

Annie blinked. 'Ah, sure.'

Mrs. Growell gave a little gasp, then put a hand over her mouth. 'I mean, Mistress. My apologies.'

Annie smiled. 'I'm quite happy with Annie,' she said. 'I'm not one for formalities. I did nothing to deserve all this.'

Mrs. Growell's face softened. 'On the contrary, I think Wilfred would have been proud of you. From what I have seen, you have all the attributes to both move this place forwards with the times, while maintaining everything he held dear.'

'Thank you. I think.'

Mrs. Growell made tea while Annie tidied up the countertops. When she returned, Mrs. Growell handed Annie a cup and said, 'Mr. Fairbrother commented that you were going through your grandfather's papers. I wondered … did you find any mention of myself?'

Annie frowned, trying to remember. 'There were a few passing references, I think. But I haven't read through them all yet.'

Mrs. Growell looked momentarily crestfallen, but quickly recovered her composure. 'Oh, I just wondered what he might have thought of his staff. He was one for the written word, after all.'

'He has dozens of diaries,' Annie said. 'I didn't even know people did that anymore.'

'He felt that the written word, like memory, expanded your life experience,' Mrs. Growell said. 'He felt that a book was only a window into a story, allowing the reader's experience to grow. A photograph or a film, on the other hand … told too much of the story, leaving nothing for the imagination.'

'It sounds like you held him in high esteem,' Annie said.

Was that a hint of a blush in Mrs. Growell's cheeks? The housekeeper gave an uncharacteristic shake of her head and poked at a strand of hair that had come out of place. 'I worked for him for many years,' she said. 'Such a feeling would therefore be … natural.'

'I think that—'

'We should box these mince pies,' Mrs. Growell said sharply. 'Mr. Fairbrother needs to drive them over to the village hall this evening.' She glanced at the floor. 'I apologise for interrupting … Miss Annie.'

Annie couldn't help but smile. She reached out and patted Mrs. Growell on the arm, feeling a momentary tensing in the older woman. 'That's quite all right.'

Mrs. Growell gave a brief nod, then looked up. 'There are, however, one or two photographs of your grandfather around,' she said. 'Mostly taken despite his reluctance, but sometimes such things are unavoidable. I will attempt to hunt them out.'

Annie smiled. 'I'd really appreciate it,' she said.

Mr. Fairbrother was out in the front garden, making a snowman with Isabella. They had found a green bed sheet and a bushel of straw somewhere to give him a cloak and a beard.

'Welcome to our castle, mighty sir,' Mr. Fairbrother said with a chuckle, as Isabella stood behind the snowman, making growling noises and waving a wooden sword about. 'Can I interest you in a chicken? Oh, hello there, Mistress Annie.'

'That's quite some snowman,' Annie said.

'We were thinking—with your permission, of course— to put on a bit of a kids snowball battle,' Mr. Fairbrother said. 'We'll need a few more, of course, but perhaps you can help with that.'

'I'd be delighted. We don't get much snow down south.'

'Bit of a microclimate here,' Mr. Fairbrother said. 'This is just a flurry.'

'Yah, yah!' Isabella said, waving her sword around.

'What's on your schedule for today?' Mr. Fairbrother asked Annie.

'Well, there's a Christmas cake decoration contest I've been asked to judge. And I have to make a speech at the opening of a remodeled kitchen in one of the restaurants. And then apparently there's a meeting about Christmas-themed fishing trips that I have to attend.'

Mr. Fairbrother grinned. 'You have to learn to say nae,' he said. 'Lord Wilf said nae to everything. After a while, they stopped asking.'

'No, no, no!' Isabella shouted, waving her sword and accidentally knocking off one of the snowman's stick arms.

Annie smiled. 'I've spent most of my adult life saying no to people wanting loans or mortgages,' she said. 'It makes a change to say yes sometimes.'

'Well, if you can hang on a couple of minutes, I'll harness up the sleigh and give you a lift. The lassie here needs to visit the toy factory and, well, I kind of had my eye on a piece of fudge or two.'

Annie had no choice but to hot chocolate and fudge her way through her newfound celebrity status in order to shake off the ongoing feeling that she was somehow unworthy. Wherever she went, people wanted to help her or give her things, offer compliments or coffee, thanks or marshmallows. While she never tired of the attention that had been almost entirely absent during her life to date, she still struggled to shake the feelings of unworthiness, that she had literally been picked off the street to live this life of stunning fortune. She never had to pay for anything, never had to queue. And people acted like she was some kind of saviour for this place of which she had only discovered a few weeks ago.

After a day of moving from one joyful event to another, she found a home for her misgivings on the quiet roads lit by old fashioned street lamps after most of the new tourists were either ensconced in the pubs and restaurants, gone back to the lodge or returned to their homes by the last train. She walked up and down the narrow streets, her hands stuffed into her pockets and her breath making plumes of steam in front of her, going over everything in her head, trying to make sense of it all.

She was just walking past the train station when a side door opened and Bill—otherwise known as Willy Whistle —stepped out and gave her a wave.

'Ah, Miss Annie. I saw you passing. Can I have a word?'

'Sure.'

Bill looked back over his shoulder and lowered his

voice. 'I'm afraid there's a man sleeping in the waiting room. This is the third night in a row. We can't have it really, you know? It'll upset the other customers.'

Annie gave a slow nod. She hadn't seen Ray Burns since the hilltop and had assumed he had gone back to Penrith. As she followed Bill up on to the platform, she saw him through the waiting room window, curled up on the bench, his jacket pulled over him.

'I've met him,' Annie said to Bill. 'Leave it with me and I'll see what I can do.'

'Okay, thanks, Miss Annie.'

As Bill went back to the station office, Annie went into the waiting room and sat down on the bench against the wall nearest to Ray's head. She was about to shake him awake, when she looked down and saw his shoes on the floor below his feet. They were water stained and damaged. One lace had broken and been tied back together.

Ray had clearly fallen on hard times. What had made him come here, Annie didn't know, but he had to have a reason for sleeping on the waiting room bench rather than head home. Perhaps he was homeless. Perhaps he had lost his job.

Instead of waking him, she lay down on the bench along the intersecting wall, cupped her hands under her head, and watched him, feeling at the same time a sense of pity and a sense of intrigue. Ray was around her age, handsome in a way, and kind. Had he suffered some kind of tragedy?

She was still wondering when the weariness of the day finally overcame her, and before she knew it, she was fast asleep.

22

A MAN IN THE GARDEN

SHE WOKE UP TO FIND A BRIGHT SUN STREAMING through the waiting room window. Annie sat up, wincing at the stiffness in her arms and legs, and looked around. Ray Burns was gone, but someone had left a fresh paper cup of coffee on the floor beside her, and she noticed how her coat had been tucked in around her legs. She smiled, then picked up the paper cup.

Someone had scrawled a message on the side: *Thanks for looking out for me. R.*

Where had he gone? Through the window, the platform was empty, the train gone. Had it already departed or not yet arrived? She wasn't familiar with the timetable yet, but Ray could have already left.

At the thought of it, Annie felt a knot of regret in her stomach. Apart from his name, and that he liked to go hiking in wildly inappropriate footwear, Annie knew nothing at all about Raymond Burns, and likely never would know.

With nothing else to do, she trudged back through a fresh layer of snow to Stone Spire Hall, where Mrs.

Growell was waiting to berate her for staying out overnight without word. Annie apologised, then joined Mr. Fairbrother—who gave her a knowing smirk—and Isabella for breakfast.

'That told you,' Mr. Fairbrother said after Mrs. Growell —having already finished—had taken her plates down to the kitchen. 'Although she was a lot nicer to you than she would have been to Lord Wilf. Would have torn strips off him.'

Isabella just sniggered behind her hand, then suddenly clicked her fingers. She lifted up a bag, then pointed up into the air. 'After breakfast,' she said, which Annie took to mean she had finished another prototype for the clockwork flying bird.

'Got it,' Annie said. Then, turning to Mr. Fairbrother, she said, 'Ah, Les … roughly how many bedrooms are there in this place?'

Mr. Fairbrother looked at the ceiling and frowned. 'Off the top of my head … seven in the west wing, five in the main building, and another seven in the east. So that's what … nineteen?'

'And how about some of those reception rooms downstairs? Could they be made into dormitories?'

'Well, I suppose they could. Why? Got some friends coming to stay?'

'Just mulling over a few ideas,' Annie said. 'I think I'd like to have school parties or disadvantaged children come here. It's a wonderful place, and I think we should share it.'

Mr. Fairbrother nodded. 'Got a couple of spare sleighs in the shed,' he said. 'Could do races.'

'Yee hah!' Isabella said, snapping a pair of imaginary reins.

'And her down there is used to cooking for big groups,' Mr. Fairbrother said.

'Really? Did she used to work in a school?'

Mr. Fairbrother smirked. 'Prison,' he said, then chuckled, leaving Annie unsure whether he was joking or not.

'Well, at least she could keep the kids in line,' Mr. Fairbrother said. 'Proper boot camp, like.'

'I was thinking of something a little more relaxed,' Annie said. 'But I suppose a bit of discipline wouldn't hurt—'

Mrs. Growell had appeared at the top of the kitchen steps. She paused to look out of the window beside the main doors, then pushed through the partition door and looked pointedly at Mr. Fairbrother.

'There's a man in the garden,' she said. 'I suggest you go out there and redirect him to the village.'

Mr. Fairbrother folded up his newspaper and headed for the main doors, Annie and Isabella following behind.

'Well, so there is,' Mr. Fairbrother said. 'I wonder what the poor chap's doing.'

Annie, leaning over Mr. Fairbrother's shoulder, let out a little gasp. On the other side of the driveway, Ray Burns was walking between snow-covered flowerbeds, head down in concentration, hands behind his back. He looked cold, confused, and more than a little lost.

'I know him,' Annie said. 'He came in on the train a few days ago, but has been sleeping in the station waiting room. Margaret, can you put some hot chocolate on and maybe make a sandwich or two? I'm not sure how well he's been eating.'

'Are you sure that offering charity to a stray is a wise decision, Mistress?'

Annie met her gaze and smiled. 'It's three weeks until Christmas,' she said. 'I think it's absolutely a wise decision.'

'Very well. As you require. Isabella, dear, would you mind giving me a hand? I'll let you slice the bread.'

'Goody goody,' Isabella said, rubbing her hands together.

'Do you want me to come with you?' Mr. Fairbrother asked.

Annie shook her head. 'No, I can handle this.'

'If you don't mind, I'll just keep an eye,' Mr. Fairbrother said. 'I'll be out in the garden, building snowmen.'

Annie put on boots, a coat, gloves and a hat, then, as an afterthought, grabbed a scarf and a spare pair of gloves for Ray, whose own seemed to have been lost. Then, with her boots crunching through the fresh snow, Annie marched out into the garden and up the path to where Ray was now standing, peering down at something in the snow.

'Um, excuse me? Ray? Are you all right?'

Ray looked up. His eyes met Annie's and he smiled. 'Oh, hello. I do apologise if I was trespassing, but there's no clear boundary marker between these gardens and the moor, and I was just following a trail. Is this where you work?'

Annie blinked. 'Oh, ah, yes, it is. That's right.'

'It's a beautiful place. Does it belong to Lord Collins?'

'It did.'

Ray gave a sad smile and looked down. 'A terrible shame.'

Annie's internal jury was still out on whether or not she agreed, having slowly got to know her grandfather from his notebooks. She just gave a noncommittal shrug.

'That's life, isn't it?'

Ray nodded. 'Yes. I suppose it is.'

His shoes were again soaking wet, and his trousers from the knees down were muddy and stained. He looked for all the world like some kind of vagabond, but in his eyes there was kindness, and his face gleamed with hope.

'Ah, did you say you were following some kind of trail?' Annie asked.

'Yes. There,' Ray said, pointing at a line of prints in the snow. 'I've been following it from beneath the Christmas tree in the square over there in the village. Isn't it a delight? I'm sure it's some kind of elf or pixie. Look at the way its pointed, as though it was someone wearing shoes. An animal would have a spread front, to indicate paws, while a bird would have toes out to the side. Plus, what bird would walk so far?'

Wondering if Ray were in fact mad, Annie said, 'I'm pretty sure it's not a fairy or an elf. Probably just a rabbit or something.'

Ray smiled. 'But wouldn't it be nice if it was?'

Annie felt a little uncomfortable under his gaze, but it was a good uncomfortable. She liked the way he looked at her, and found herself saying, 'Why don't you come up to the house? Your shoes are soaked. I'm sure we can find some for you to wear. And I'll ask the housekeeper to make you something to eat.'

'Are you sure?'

'Come on.'

Annie headed back to the house, looking back over her shoulder every few steps, on the pretence of checking to see if Ray was following, but really just to see if he was … well, following. That was all.

He's not really suitable boyfriend material, Annie. Even if you're sitting at the bottom of the barrel yourself.

'Hello lad,' Mr. Fairbrother called, as they passed where he was fashioning a lump of recently shoveled snow into a vague pillar shape. 'Nice to see you again.'

'You've met?' Annie said.

'Was casting my line off the pier last evening,' Mr. Fairbrother said. 'We had a craic for a few.'

'Did you catch anything in the end?' Ray asked.

Mr. Fairbrother chuckled. 'Not sure. The ice froze up again around my line so I left it down there. Could be a whopper hanging on it, for all I know. I'll pop down later and have a look.'

'If there is, perhaps get a stone fire burning down there by the waterside,' Ray said. 'Would taste fantastic.'

'There's a plan,' Mr. Fairbrother said.

Annie glanced at Ray. There was something strangely nostalgic in the way he spoke, sepia-tinted, almost sad. Shaking off the feeling, she said, 'Come on, Ray. Let's get you warm, dry, and fed.'

Annie led him into the house, then instructed him to take off his shoes and socks. Mr. Fairbrother kept a box of thick, winter socks by the door, presumably to change when he came inside, and Annie figured he wouldn't mind if she lent a pair to Ray. His trousers were still wet, but after he had dried them with a towel, they would last until Annie had time to find him some others.

She had just sat him down at their usual breakfast table in front of a fire Mr. Fairbrother had recently stoked, when Mrs. Growell and Isabella came up the stairs. Mrs. Growell carried a plate of sandwiches, Isabella a large teapot, which, from the smell, was filled with hot chocolate.

'Oh,' Ray said. 'Has your family served the Collinses for a while then?'

'Whatever do you mean?'

'Well, that's your mother and daughter, right? I can see the resemblance.'

Annie winced, but luckily Mrs. Growell and Isabella hadn't heard. 'We're all unrelated,' she said, although, even as she said it, she felt a tingle on her tongue as though in some way, it was perhaps a lie. Isabella, for one thing, did look like a much younger, slightly more pixiefied, easygoing version of Mrs. Growell, and she—

'Your daughter has your eyes,' Ray said.

'She's not my daughter,' Annie almost snapped, getting the words out just before Mrs. Growell and Isabella came into earshot, but getting a stern glare from Mrs. Growell anyway as the housekeeper looked Ray up and down with a look of disdain, as though she'd just found a drowned rat lying on the front doorstep.

'Sandwiches,' she said.

'And hot chocolate,' Isabella chimed in, grinning wildly.

'Ah, Mrs.—ah, Margaret, do you think we could find a change of clothes for Ray here? He's a little wet.'

'Certainly. I'll have a look in the closet.'

As Mrs. Growell set down the sandwiches and marched off, Ray said, 'Wow, you have her under your thumb. Anyone would think you owned this place.'

Isabella began to giggle. Annie felt her cheeks flush. 'Ah, I suppose, technically I do. I'm … ah, Wilfred Collins's granddaughter.'

Ray's reaction was immediate and unexpected. He had been sitting in a chair, but now he knelt down on the floor, clasping his hands together as though to pray, and looked up at Annie with tears in his eyes.

'Your grandfather was a wonderful man,' he said. 'And in his absence, I'd just like to thank you for making a poor man extremely happy.'

'Marry?' Isabella said.

'I don't think Ray means it like that,' Annie said. 'Uh, Ray, can you get up, please? What's going on?'

Ray stood up, his eyes not leaving Annie's. He sat back

down on the chair, took a sip of hot chocolate from a mug Isabella had filled, then smiled.

'A long time ago, there was a very poor man,' he said. 'His wife had died unexpectedly, leaving him to bring up his young son on his own. They had very little money, but they got by, because the man loved the boy very much. However, the boy got sick. Very sick. The boy was going to die without a special kind of treatment that wasn't available in his own country, but the man had no money to send the boy overseas. The man tried everything, but he was one of the little people, between the cracks, the type no one really cares about. He got turned down for grants, turned down for loans. Letters to prominent public figures were ignored, and attempts to fundraise were met with apathy. With no other choice, he sold everything he had of value, but it still wasn't enough. In short, he had no way to save the boy.'

Isabella was nibbling her fingernails, eyes wide. Annie wiped away a tear.

'What happened?' she asked.

'The man, perhaps in desperation, perhaps because he was drunk or had gone crazy through grief, did the only thing he could think of that he hadn't yet tried, something so ridiculous he would surely have laughed at himself in other circumstances.'

'What?' Annie asked.

'What? What? *What?*' Isabella echoed.

Ray gave a sad chuckle. 'He wrote a letter to Father Christmas.'

'No!'

'Nooo!'

'Yes. And then he forgot about it, and set about trying to make the boy comfortable in his last days. Not wanting to miss a single second, the man quit his job, and spent his days with his son, wanting to bag every memory he could. And then, from nowhere, a miracle happened. Father Christmas wrote back.'

'No!'

'Nooooo!'

'What did he say?'

'The letter, addressed directly to the man and his son, talked about how it was important to believe and never to give up. To stay strong, and to have hope, and to know that magic existed in the world, and that magic could do anything if you only believed in it strongly enough. It was, in short inspirational.'

'And that saved the boy? His self-belief?'

'*Noooooooo!*'

Ray smiled. 'Not quite, but it helped him stay positive through everything. The letter also contained a cheque for two hundred grand.'

'What?' Annie gasped.

Isabella clapped her hands together and started laughing.

'Father Christmas's very generous donation helped that boy get the treatment he needed, and he not only survived, but he went from strength to strength. And the man's desperate prayer was answered, because he never, ever gave up.'

Isabella sniffed. Annie glanced at her to see that the girl had tears streaming down her face.

'That's amazing,' Annie said. 'And that man was you?'

Ray, his own eyes filled with tears, smiled as he shook his head. 'No,' he said. 'I was the boy.'

23

AN AWKWARD HOUSE GUEST

THE MAN WHO HAD DISAPPEARED OUT OF HER FAMILY'S life after an argument with his son now appeared in a completely different light. Alone in her grandfather's rooms, by checking dates to find out when he had made his Christmas donation to Raymond's father, Annie recognised how to find others. While he had waxed lyrical about his attempts to discover the supposed real magic out in the surrounding forest, on the occasions when he had offered his own more secular—but in Annie's opinion, no less worthy—version, he had made only brief, blink-and-you'll-miss-them notes, perhaps to remind himself, but certainly never to be read by anyone else.

Sent another letter this morning to a young lady from Dorset whose parents required a present that was a little extra special. Fingers crossed next year a doll will suffice.

A little boy wished for his hair back for Christmas. This year might be pushing it, but by next, all being well.

Walking in the snow rather than sitting by the window watching her friends … not an easy one to fulfill but perhaps with a little something extra in her stocking this year….

Increasingly able to spot them, Annie counted dozens of other such cryptic messages. There was no other information to go on, no names, addresses, rarely even mention of any specific illness, but they went on and on, right up to last Christmas, and even up into the days before his death:

Old Beardy put something in the mail for a group of needy kids in Edinburgh this morning. The old guy can't deliver decent parents, but a swimming pool might ease their troubles, if it's done by next summer.

By the time she closed the last diary, Annie was wiping tears from her eyes. She put the book away, closed the drawer and went downstairs.

Mrs. Growell greeted her in the hallway.

'Mistress Annie, I must ask how long are you planning to allow the man to stay? I found him in the armoury this afternoon, waiving around one of your grandfather's antique swords.'

'How much are they worth?' Annie said. 'Can we sell them?'

Mrs. Growell's eyes flared. 'Mistress, your grandfather would be distraught at the very thought. Many of those weapons were discovered on archeological digs he himself funded. It was something of a hobby.'

Annie frowned. 'Is there a museum in the village?'

'Not that I'm aware of.'

'Then I think it's time we had the, um, elves build one.

There's far too much old stuff sitting around in Grandfather's house, unseen by the outside world.'

Mrs. Growell let out a humph. 'Why don't you just open the house to tourists?'

'I very well might,' Annie said, holding the housekeeper's gaze and getting a look of horror for her troubles.

'Your grandfather liked to keep the outside world at bay,' Mrs. Growell said in a hollow voice. 'He was a very private person.'

'I'm not sure you knew my grandfather as well as you think you did,' Annie said. 'I think he would have liked for people to have come to this house. And anyway, it's technically mine now.'

As Mrs. Growell forced a respectful nod before marching off, Annie found herself almost immediately regretting her words. Of course Mrs. Growell knew her grandfather better; she had lived and worked with him her whole life. Annie had thought him dead for the last twenty years.

Mrs. Growell had retreated to her kitchen fortress, so it was too late to apologise now. Instead, Annie headed upstairs to the second floor, where she knocked lightly on a guest bedroom door.

'Just one moment.'

The sounds of movement came from behind the door, then it opened to reveal Ray, cleaned and groomed, dressed in some clothes that Les had donated. The shirt cuffs and jeans were a little short, but he looked like a different man to the one Annie had seen shuffling around the village and the house grounds. He looked happy, radiant, even. And with the colour restored to his face, he even looked handsome.

'Sorry about that, I was just tidying up.'

'Are you feeling better?'

Ray nodded. 'Much. Thank you. I appreciate you putting me up. I'll be gone in a day or two, I promise. I think I'm ready now.'

Annie felt a sudden pang of longing in the pit of her stomach, but she barely knew the man; to mention it would be more forward than she could handle. Instead, she just said, 'Oh, well, if that's what you need to do....'

Ray nodded. 'I just had to come here and pay my respects to your grandfather's memory. Thanks to him, my father died a happy, contented man.'

Annie's eyes filled with tears. 'I'm ... I'm glad.'

'If there were others like me whom he helped, there's no doubt he made a lot of lives better. Are you all right?'

Annie nodded. 'I'm sorry,' she said. 'It's just that everything you told me ... it was a bit of a revelation. You see, I didn't know my grandfather at all. I thought he died years ago.'

'Really?'

'He didn't get along with my dad. I don't really know what happened.'

Ray smiled. 'Sometimes, we can't always define why one person gets along with another, or not, as the case may be. It can be that two seemingly stable people just don't fit. And then you'll have others that you wouldn't think would fit in a million years be blissfully happy together.'

Annie frowned. 'What was it you said you did?'

'Oh, I don't do anything now. I quit my job.'

'But ... before?'

Ray smiled again. 'I was a professor of philosophy at a university.'

'Oh, wow.'

Ray shrugged. 'That probably explains all the weird things that come out of my mouth.'

'Why did you, uh, quit?'

'It's a long story.' Ray looked down at his feet. 'Thanks again for letting me stay. I'll be out by Wednesday at the latest.'

'It's all right, I'm sure Mrs. Growell won't mind. Just … ah, please stay out of the armoury.'

'Sorry about that. I think I scared her.'

'If that's possible, yeah.'

Aware the corridor was a little chilly, Annie stuffed her hands into her pockets. Ray was still looking at her with that kind, easy smile, and she figured, screw it, it was Christmas. If you couldn't take a chance at Christmas, when could you?

'Ah … I imagine you're hungry,' she said, even though they'd only had breakfast an hour before. 'If you haven't checked out the shops in Undercastle yet, do you want to go get a pancake or some fudge?'

Ray lifted an eyebrow. 'Or both?'

Annie smiled. 'Merry Christmas,' she said.

'Oh my god, you moved him in already? What happened to all that no more men after Troy business?'

'It's not like that!' Annie said, blushing at Julie's words. 'Nothing's happened. We just had some fudge, and some pancakes, and then a couple of hot chocolates, and it was … nice.'

'Just nice?'

'Well … you know how when you go out with someone and the time just flies, and every time you glance at the clock like half an hour's gone by, and you wish it would slow down … it was like that.'

'Oh my god, you're besotted. So, just to clarify, this is some homeless, unemployed philosopher you found sleeping in the train station and whom you moved into your giant manor house without knowing anything about him?'

'That's it, in a nutshell.'

'Is his room on the same floor?'

'Along the corridor. I don't think we've gone that far, though.'

'Aren't you worried that he might be a freeloader?'

'Well, I think that's what Mrs. Growell thinks.'

'The housekeeper?'

'Yeah. I don't know though. I thought he was having some kind of mental breakdown, because he was happy enough to sleep on benches and wander about in the snow with his shoes soaking wet. When I asked him, he got all cryptic, and asked me if I knew how it felt.'

'How what felt?'

'How it felt to wake up on a bench in a train station. Or to walk in the snow with wet shoes. And just this morning, on the way back, he decided he wanted to climb a tree.'

'What?'

'Yeah. So we went into the forest a bit until we found one that was just right, and then up he went. And he didn't just climb it, but he went really high, way higher than I thought was safe, right up to where the branches weren't strong enough to hold him. He must have been five or six metres off the ground. And do you know what he did then?'

'He fell out?'

'No, nothing like that. He started laughing. And then he asked me to come up.'

'And?'

'So I did. It was absolutely terrifying, but at the same time … thrilling.'

Julie chuckled. 'Are you sure he's not got some kind of mental problem? He sounds downright wacko.'

'I think it's the philosophy thing. He keeps talking about how we coast through life without ever really pushing ourselves. He said we should make every day an entirely new experience.'

'Easy enough to say, isn't it? It doesn't sound like he has kids.'

'No, he's never mentioned any. Or a wife.'

'So it's a clear run through to goal, then, is it?'

'I didn't say that! If he's not married, perhaps there's something wrong with him.'

'You're not married.'

'Yeah, but—'

'And you're divorced, which is a double black mark.'

'Ha. Thanks for the vote of confidence.'

'I didn't mean it like that. All I'm saying is that you don't know his circumstances. They could be anything.'

Annie couldn't help but smile. 'It's a voyage of discovery, isn't it?'

Annie had eaten so much fudge that she wasn't sure she could handle dinner. When Mrs. Growell appeared with a full joint of roast beef, however, she figured she could squeeze a little more down. Tomorrow, she would need to compensate with a morning run up to the top of the hill to ease her guilt.

Mrs. Growell set down the dining platter and clasped her hands over her stomach. 'Will your … friend be joining us for dinner, Mistress?'

'Yes, I asked him,' Annie said. 'But he's late.'

'Well, don't let the food get cold. Mr. Fairbrother, I'm placing you on carving duties.'

She handed him a carving knife and a fork, then turned and marched off.

Mr. Fairbrother chuckled. 'Didn't take her out of the freezer early enough,' he said, throwing a glance at the kitchen stairs. 'She's a little frostier than usually this evening.'

'She's not happy about Ray staying,' Annie said.

'It's your house,' Mr. Fairbrother answered. 'Although she probably thinks it's hers.'

Annie said nothing. She had been thinking the same thing. While she doubted Mrs. Growell was ever particularly joyful, she was beginning to sympathise with the housekeeper's situation.

'I'll talk to her,' she said. *Although I'm not sure what I'll say.*

'Good evening,' came a voice from the doorway.

Annie looked up to see Ray, dressed in a smart suit and tie, walking across the room. He had combed his hair and looked like James Bond. Annie couldn't bring herself to answer, even as Isabella giggled and muttered, 'Penguin,' under her breath.

'I hope you don't mind me borrowing this old suit,' Ray said as he approached the table. 'I opened a cupboard in my guestroom and there were about thirty of them. I had to try on a couple before I found one that fit.'

'You look—'

'Like lightning in a bottle,' Mr. Fairbrother said.

'Bazaam!' Isabella shouted, making a wild piano motion with her fingers.

'Ah, thanks. I've never worn a suit quite like this before.'

'Please sit down.'

Raymond pulled out a chair between Isabella and Annie and sat down. He was just smoothing out his trousers when a sudden cry of alarm came from the other side of the room. Annie looked up just in time to see Mrs. Growell, coming through the door, throw up her hands and send a tray of potatoes sailing through the air. As she cupped her face, eyes wide with shock, the potatoes crashed down like a meteor shower on the hard stone floor. With one more wide-eyed gasp of utter horror, Mrs. Growell turned and fled, the door banging closed behind her.

Mr. Fairbrother was the first to act, leaping out of his chair like a man half his age, scooping up what potatoes hadn't exploded and piling them back on the tray.

'I cleaned this floor yesterday morning so we can make it a ten second rule instead of five,' he muttered, stuffing one half-crushed potato into his mouth before returning with a tray of salvaged remains.

Isabella had run to a cupboard behind the door and retrieved a dustpan and brush. 'I'll help you,' Annie said, but Mr. Fairbrother shook his head.

'Me, the lassie, and the lad here will finish cleaning up. You'd better go and see what's up with her downstairs.'

Facing a distraught Mrs. Growell was the least desired of the available options, but technically as lady of the house Annie figured she had no choice. She left the others to clean up and headed downstairs.

There was no sign of Mrs. Growell in the kitchens. Annie called her name, but got no answer, so began trying doors instead. It was only now that she realised how little she had explored of the house's basements, as she opened doors and peered into rooms she hadn't even known existed. Most of them were stacked with old tables and chairs, but near the end of a gloomy service corridor she came to one with a thin strip of light along the bottom.

With a polite knock, Annie called out, 'Mrs. Growell? Margaret? Are you in there?'

At first she thought she must be mistaken, but then heard a shuffling sound on the other side of the door. It opened slowly to reveal Mrs. Growell's face. At the sight of Annie, Mrs. Growell lifted a hand and wiped away a tear, then gave a shake of her head.

'Forgive me, Mistress, but I had a bit of a turn back there.'

'Are you all right?'

Mrs. Growell looked down. 'For a moment there I thought I saw a ghost.'

'A ghost?'

'That man. He was wearing one of your grandfather's suits. I haven't seen those used since … well, for a long time.'

'I can ask him to take it off if you like.'

Mrs. Growell shook her head. 'No, dear, I mean, Mistress. It's all right. I will just have to steel myself.'

Annie stepped back but Mrs. Growell made no move to close the door. She continued to stare at the floor as though reliving memories in the swirls of the old carpet.

'Margaret, why don't you take the evening off? Or even a few days if you'd like. Perhaps you could visit some friends or something?'

Mrs. Growell shook her head. 'My life is here. Forgive me, Mistress. Give me five minutes to compose myself, then I shall return to my duties.'

And with that, she went back inside the room and closed the door with a soft thud.

24

REBIRTH

'Okay,' Isabella said, facing into the wind. 'Ready? Launch!'

Annie threw the clockwork bird into the air. Its wings caught in the wind, and it began to jerk back and forth. Isabella lifted her musical instrument and frantically began to tap something reminiscent of an eighties TV theme song. Annie watched the bird right itself, flap a couple of times, then suddenly dip and nosedive into the snow.

Isabella giggled and shrugged. 'Next time.'

'That was close, wasn't it?' Annie said. 'We nearly had it.'

'Close,' Isabella agreed. Then, with another giggle, she scooped the bird out of the snow, brushed it down, and put it back into a bag. Looking up at Annie, she said, 'Modifications.'

'Right. Do you need any help?'

Isabella shook her head. 'Nope.'

'I'm going to head down into the village, then.'

Isabella raised a hand and made an okay gesture. 'Okay,' she added, just in case.

Diane was wiping tables in the pancake house when Annie entered. A young couple sat at one of the tables, leaning forward, hands entwined. At another table, an older man had his head slumped to the side and was snoring loudly.

'He looks full,' Annie said, nodding towards him.

Diane laughed. 'He ate three double cream cheese and chocolate pancakes. He did the same thing yesterday too. Slept for half an hour, then woke up to get lunch. Are you going to the ice sculpture competition this afternoon?'

Annie smiled. 'I'm one of the judges. This is so exciting. I don't know anything about ice sculptures. Mr. Fairbrother made breakfast for me this morning by way of a bribe. He said he's got one in the competition.'

'Oh dear.'

'Which means, for fairness, no matter how good it is, I have to pick someone else. Luckily there are five other judges and the prize is only a book of coupons for free ice-cream, and a little trophy.'

'Oh dear, well, it wouldn't be good for him to win the coupons anyway. I've worried about his cholesterol for years. What was he doing making breakfast?'

'Mrs. Growell called in sick. Well, called up, from her basement rooms.'

Diane's eyes widened. 'No! Margaret never gets sick. Like, literally never. It must be something else.'

'Yeah … I let a man stay in the house.'

She briefly explained about Ray. Diane listened, wide-eyed, then at the end, chuckled and gave Annie's forearm a shake.

'And you moved him in already? You wicked thing. We've been wondering how long you would stay single.'

'What? Who's we?'

'Oh, just me and a few of the other residents. What you'd call the M.C.G.C., the morning coffee gossip circle. When you showed up single, we wondered how long it would be before you found someone.' She clapped her hands together. 'When's the wedding? I love a royal wedding.'

'Ah, there's not going to be a wedding, and I'm most certainly not royal. I'm a bank clerk.'

'You were a bank clerk. Now you're the lady of the manor, which for us local paupers makes you practically royalty.'

'I'm actually still officially a bank clerk. I'm on holiday. I need to call my boss.'

'You're going to quit and move up here permanently, I assume?'

'Well, I don't know.'

'Oh, go on. What have you got to lose?'

'Well, my....'

Annie trailed off. There was Julie, of course. She'd miss her best friend. And then there was the bakery up the street where she sometimes bought a sandwich on a Saturday morning … and there was …well, a decent park that she sometimes walked in….

'I might move up here permanently,' she said. 'Please tell me it's a little warmer in the summer.'

'Oh, it's delightful,' Diane said. 'Christmas is the best, though. Even without the tourists, it was magical. This year, it'll be the most magical of all.'

'I can't wait.'

'And what better way to celebrate than with a new man on your arm?'

Annie grimaced. 'I've been married, and it sucked. I mean, it started off all right, but it only took a couple of years before I realised I'd made a mistake. And then of course, there were the five years or so we stayed together kind of deluding ourselves that we hadn't made a mistake, followed by the fall out and the divorce, and him somehow managing to come out better and screwing me out of everything.' Annie looked up and grinned. 'Merry Christmas.'

'Not all men are pigs,' Diane said. 'My Jonathan was a wonderful man. He died of a heart attack halfway up Snowdon. Loved the outdoors, he did.'

'I'm so sorry.'

Diane smiled. 'Don't be. He died the way he lived, full of adventure. It was after he died that I moved here, looking for an adventure of my own. And thanks to you, I'm finally having one. There's this man who's been in three times this week, and each time he sits at the counter with his pancake, just to talk to me.'

'I hope it works out.'

Diane laughed. 'It may or may not. That's life, isn't it? But if you don't live it, you'll never know.'

'I wish I could get Mrs. Growell to live a little,' Annie said. 'I mean, she rarely smiles, and she lives like a mouse in a hole.'

'Margaret was dedicated to your grandfather,' Diane said. 'I don't think you really understand how much. She worshiped him but also worried for him in equal measure. She was both his wife and mother at the same time.'

'Isn't that a little weird?'

Diane let out a sudden howl of laughter that made the young couple sit up and the snoring man jerk awake. 'Oh, dear!' she cried. 'I mean, metaphorically.'

As the customers settled back down—the young couple to gaze into each other's eyes and the snoring man back into his doze, Diane patted Annie on the arm again.

'Try not to worry too much about Mrs. Growell,' she

said. 'In her way, she's happy. Worry about yourself. So …
tell me more about this man?'

Annie shrugged. 'To be honest, I still don't know that
much about him.'

'Well, what are you waiting for? Why don't you go and
find out?'

Ray had left after breakfast to go to Undercastle, saying he
wanted to look around the shops again. As Annie picked
her way through the laughing, smiling tourists, she looked
through shop windows and doors, but found no sign of
him. In the little village square she found Brian Ackerley,
a.k.a Bunty Glitterbottom, making balloon animals for a
group of smiling children.

'And this is an alpaca,' he said, handing a twist of white
balloons to one little boy.

'It looks like a llama,' another boy said.

'Give it a name and it can be whatever you want,'
Brian said, catching sight of Annie and giving her a wink.
'Even an albino giraffe.'

'His name's Alan!' the first boy cried. 'Alan Alpaca!'

'Nice,' Brian said, all the while his hands working on
the next creation. Finishing it as Annie reached him, he
handed it to a little girl wearing pink earmuffs and said,
'Here you are, dear. A giant panda.'

As the girl squealed with delight and headed off with
her parents, Brian turned to Annie. 'Hello there, Miss. Can
I make you a balloon dolphin or something?'

'I'm looking for someone,' Annie said. 'He's called Ray
Burns. Did you hear about the man sleeping in the train
station waiting room?'

'Oh, him,' Brian said. 'Willy Whistle told me about

him. Yeah, he was here earlier. He wanted me to show him how to make a balloon starfish. It was quite the challenge, but we had a good try.'

'Do you know where he went?'

'He was heading down to the lakeside.'

'All right, thanks.'

Brian gave his elf hat a little lift. 'Are you sure I can't interest you in a balloon monkey? Maybe even just a cat or dog?'

'Maybe later,' Annie said.

She left Bunty to his balloons as a school group appeared out of a chocolate shop, and headed down to the lakeside. A wooden pier extended out into the water, but the handful of boats had been dragged up onto the shore as the inlet was now completely covered in ice. Several people were skating inside an arc of cones placed to identify the area where the ice was safe.

There was no sign of Ray, but as Annie wandered among the boats that likely floated around the lake during the summer months, she spotted a line of tracks heading off, angling along the shoreline and out of sight around a low hill.

Surely not…?

She was wearing boots just tall enough for the ankle-deep snow. Following the tracks, she trudged along the shoreline until Undercastle was out of sight behind her. The hill, moorland in summer, rose to a low peak, then dipped down again into an area of trees. The path moved away from the lakeside for a while, cutting through the trees, until it crossed a rocky, fast moving stream—a "beck", she remembered Mr. Fairbrother telling her they were called in the Lake District. Under the trees the water had stayed clear of snow, and while patches of ice covered the pools, the middle part of it still flowed quickly. Annie paused for a moment, hearing what sounded like rocks striking other rocks, then headed up a path that followed the line of the beck as it rose into the forest.

Under the trees, much of the ground was clear, so she didn't see the tracks until she came to a clearing where the river was wider, flowing into a pretty, round pool before continuing on down the hill. Ray was near the beck, taking rocks from one side of the pool and building a dam along the pool's edge to make it deeper. As he lowered a rock into place and rose up, he caught sight of her, let out a little gasp of surprise, and then smiled.

'What on earth are you doing?' Annie said.

Ray grinned. 'I'm just deepening the pool a little.'

'Whatever for?'

'I want to take a swim. Isn't it lovely here?' He gestured around him at the trees and the little waterfall that was feeding the pool. 'It's idyllic. I couldn't have imagined a better place for a quick dip.'

'You're joking, right? It's December, and it's absolutely freezing.'

Ray grinned again. 'I know. It's perfect.'

'You're out of your mind.'

Ray nodded. 'For sure. Are you coming in?'

'No!'

Ray shrugged. 'Up to you. I'll only be a couple of minutes.' And with that, he began to unbutton his coat, seemingly oblivious to her standing a mere few steps away. She turned away, looking back into the forest, but as she heard him dropping his clothes down onto a rock he had cleared of snow, she couldn't help but glance back.

He had left his underwear on. She wouldn't have

described him as muscular, more lean, without any hint of fat. Why he wasn't freezing was anyone's guess.

As he stepped into the water, he let out a little gasp. 'Wow, cold. Oh, wow. That's really, really cold.'

Annie turned, feeling unashamed. Ray had waded into the middle and sat down, the water up to his shoulders. He glanced up at Annie and gave a half grimace, half smile.

'This is something else,' he said. 'If you want to join me, you've got about half a minute before I give up. Come on, Annie. It'll make you feel alive, trust me. So, so alive.'

There was a conviction to his words that cajoled Annie into action. If a philosopher couldn't tell her the meaning of life, then no one could. And what did it really matter what anyone thought? She was in the middle of the woods, in the middle of winter, in the middle of the most bizarre few weeks of her entire life.

Why on earth not?

'Close your eyes,' she said. 'Or, keep them open. It's up to you.'

Ray smiled. 'I'll pretend not to look,' he said.

'Don't get excited,' Annie said. 'I'm not exactly a gym bunny.'

Although she had always eaten well and looked after herself, except while in the middle of her marriage breakup, where she had sometimes drank and comfort-ate herself into oblivion. A couple of years of walking to work in order to save on petrol had gone some way to repairing that, but she also wasn't getting any younger.

The air was like a blanket of ice as she pulled off her clothes, stripping down to her underwear. Her stomach felt a little loose—thanks mostly to Mrs. Growell's excellent cooking, and far too many afternoon pancake or fudge trips—but the cold air seemed to squeeze her, tighten her into something carved out of ice. She laid her clothes on a clear rock and made her way down to the water, wincing with each step as the frozen ground sent tingles of cold racing up her legs. She could only imagine how cold the water was, and was certain she would chicken out, but as she reached the pool's edge, Ray smiled.

'You'll never look at life the same,' he said, his voice sounding a little strained as he forced a smile. 'Trust me. Hurry up, though eh. I think my toes are starting to break off.'

'I must be out of my mind,' Annie said, dipping the toes of one foot into the water and wincing at the cold. It wasn't just cold, it was numbingly cold. It felt like if she stepped into the water, she would turn into ice and never be able to get back out.

'Sometimes being out of it is better than being in it,' Ray said. Then, dropping the philosophical tone, he added, 'Come on, quick. I think I'm shutting down.'

Annie took a deep breath. 'All right. Here goes. You're mad, Ray. But maybe that's a good thing.'

She closed her eyes, gritted her teeth and stepped forward, willing the water to come up and surround her to save her needing to make the decision for herself. And suddenly she was up to her neck, her entire body throbbing, every inch of skin tingling, as the cold ran through her as though she were a sieve, leaving her barely able to breathe. She looked at Ray and tried to speak, but her bottom lip was trembling so much that words wouldn't come out.

'I th ... th ... think ... I'm ... d ... d ... dying.'

Ray shook his head. 'You're not dying,' he said. 'You're living.'

And Annie knew he was right. She let go of the fear and her nerves, and embraced the shock of the cold, feeling the freezing water moving around her, chilling every part of her body.

'And now the best bit,' Ray said.

With a smile, he stood up, wading quickly out of the water. His body was pale, lean, the muscles more pronounced. He looked young, alive, powerful. Like he could take on the world and win. Only the look in his eyes told her something else.

She managed to last a few more seconds before the cold became too much, and she stood up too, moving to the side of the pool where Ray handed her a towel he had taken from a bag. She saw he had several, as though he planned repeated visits over the course of the day.

'How do you feel?' he asked.

'C … c … cold,' Annie stammered.

'Wait for it,' Ray said.

And then, as he said it, her body began to *plume*. Heat filled her as her blood reacted to the shock of the cold, making her skin prickle. She felt clean, awake, alive, vital … reborn even.

'Ray … thank you,' she gasped. She felt almost drunk, but in a good way, as though she were drunk on life, and before she could understand what she was doing, she had reached out and squeezed his hand.

With his fingers in hers, he looked at her and gave a sad smile. Then, giving her fingers a quick return squeeze, he let them go, then turned away, drying himself, quickly pulling his clothes back on.

As Annie did the same, drying herself as best she could, quickly pulling off her wet underwear while Ray's back was turned and pulling the rest of her clothes back on before wrapping her underwear in her towel, she watched his back, wondering. There was something about him….

Dressed again, he turned to her and smiled. 'Well, that

was something, wasn't it? You should do it again sometime.'

No mention of doing it together.

'Ray,' Annie said, watching him, holding his gaze. 'Are you all right?'

He gave a sad smile. 'I'm afraid not,' he said. 'The old sickness. It took a while, but eventually it came back. And this time it's not going to go away.'

25

PROMISES AND GOODBYES

SHE FELT LIKE HER HEART WAS BROKEN SO BADLY IT could never be repaired. Ray didn't want to talk about what was wrong with him, instead filling the awkward silences with whimsical, philosophical inanities, interspersed with soliloquies about how much he loved this area, how happy he was to be here. Annie was more circumspect, the euphoria she had briefly felt grounded almost before it had taken flight. In a moment she had thought Ray might be the man of her dreams, only to learn in the next that the man of her dreams would perhaps soon be nothing more than that: a dream, or a memory.

Ray, for his part, refused to give in to the misery Annie felt. His smile was constant, his words always positive and filled with a simple joy. Life was good, he reminded her. Enjoy every second, every moment.

On returning to Undercastle, Ray insisted on a pancake and a large hot chocolate to 'replenish the fuel tanks.' Diane, wearing a knowing smile, kept trying to catch Annie's eye, while all the while Annie felt emptier and emptier inside.

The ice sculpture competition briefly cheered her up. Annie's fears about having to place Mr. Fairbrother proved unfounded as the caretaker's effort—allegedly a potato, but Annie couldn't really differentiate it from any other vaguely oval-shaped object—was some way down the placings. Won by a sixteen-year-old from Edinburgh with a pretty decent attempt at a reindeer—despite one antler unfortunately breaking off—Annie headed back to Stone Spire Hall with a sense of fulfillment.

When she arrived, however, a feeling of despondency clouded over her again. Ray had returned early, saying he needed to pack his bags, as he planned to leave early in the morning. Annie felt like her world had bloomed and then died all in the space of a few hours.

Mr. Fairbrother was alone in the entrance hall when she arrived, reading his newspaper in front of the fire. There was no sign of Isabella or Mrs. Growell.

'I just saw your friend,' he said, chuckling. 'We had a mock sword fight in the armoury. Don't tell Marge or she'll use one of those rusty old things to gut me and put me on tomorrow's dinner platter. He's an odd one, isn't he? You know, he asked me if we'd ever abseiled down from the roof. When I told him not that I could remember, he asked me why not?'

Annie smiled. 'Why don't we try it tomorrow?' she said. 'After Ray ... Ray's ... gone.'

She coughed the last word then immediately started to cry. Mr. Fairbrother folded his newspaper and stood up, his arms outstretched.

'Don't cry,' he said.

Annie glared at him. 'Instead of standing there waiting

to catch a ball, I could really do with a hug right about now,' she said.'

Mr. Fairbrother inched forward. 'Oh, well, I suppose, but you're the boss.'

'And I'm also upset!' Annie wailed, a little more dramatically than she had planned, but it had the desired effect. Mr. Fairbrother stepped forward and pulled her into a warm, fatherly hug.

'There there,' he said, 'No need to cry, love. Huh, reminds me of one of my little ones with a skinned knee or after a fall off the bike.'

'Little ones? You have kids?'

Mr. Fairbrother nodded. 'Yeah, three. Kim, Mike and Beth. Kim and Mike live in London. Beth, my youngest, is off at university in Edinburgh.' Annie felt rather than saw him grin. 'Fourth year of a dentistry course. Such a clever thing. Takes after her mother, brainy old mare. She ran off with a chemistry teacher when they were kids. Brought them up myself.'

Annie pulled away. 'I had no idea you had a family or children.'

'Brought them up in my cottage over there by the lake,' Mr. Fairbrother said. 'They used to knock about in the woods with Isabella. I think there's a lot you don't know, Mistress.' He grinned. 'But that's life, isn't it? One big long river.' He chuckled. 'The longer the better. Although I might have to lay off the fudge a bit to keep mine going.'

Annie smiled. 'You're doing okay,' she said.

'And what about you?'

'I don't know.'

'Well, why don't you go up and have a chat with young Ray up there. He said he's got to leave, but who knows, maybe he'll come back.' Then, with another chuckle, he added, 'Just don't get up to any shenanigans up there, or she'll know. You might not think she does, but she does. She knows everything.'

'All right,' Annie said. 'Thanks for the tip. Have you seen Margaret today?'

Mr. Fairbrother sighed and shook his head. 'Nae. Still hiding in her room. Something's up with her. Dinner might have to be beans on toast.'

'I'll go and talk to her.'

Mr. Fairbrother shook his head. 'She's not going anywhere. Go and see to your young man first. She'll still be there when he's gone, trust me.'

'Thank you, Les.'

'All part of the job, Mistress Annie,' he said. 'My job description is caretaker, after all, isn't it?' He lowered his voice as he added, 'And between you and me, I prefer you over old Lord Wilf anyway. A right scrooge with the Christmas bonus, he was.'

Annie smiled and patted Mr. Fairbrother on the shoulder. 'Thanks, Les,' she said. 'Thanks for everything.'

Outside Ray's room, Annie steeled herself before knocking. She had no idea what she would say when he opened the door, but he didn't give her long to think about it, the door swinging open to reveal his smiling face.

'Annie?'

'Hi, Ray. Can I come in?'

'It's your house, so technically you don't need to ask, but since you did, of course.'

He stepped back as Annie came into the room. All Ray's belongings sat in a neat pile on a desk by the window. The bed was neatly made, and everything was tidy. He could have blinked out of existence and left no trace of his parting. At the thought of it, Annie choked down a sob.

'I don't want you to go,' she said.

Ray cocked his head. 'I have to,' he said. 'I have to see my specialist in a couple of days, so I have to get going. I just needed to come here … before….'

'I mean, I don't want you to … die.'

'We all have to die eventually.'

'Yes, but most of us end up crusty and old like my grandfather so that when we die we'll have no regrets.'

'Ah, you will have. You'll always have regrets. What you're looking for is a net gain. If you can die with more happy memories than sad, you can consider it a life well lived.'

Annie lifted her hands and pressed her fists against his chest. 'Can you please stop talking like a philosophy textbook? I'm being emotional here. What I'm saying is that even though I've only known you a few days, and the first time I met you, you were sleeping rough on a bench in the train station, and the second time you had soaking wet shoes, because you hadn't even bothered to wrap plastic bags over them—'

'I would have slipped over—'

'And you make me climb trees and sit in pools of freezing water, and you want to abseil off the roof—'

'It was a general enquiry, I'd have to check it for safety—'

'And just shut up before I cry even more.'

Ray smiled. 'I've left quite the impression on you, haven't I?'

Annie looked up into his eyes. For a long time she couldn't say anything. Then, at last, she said, 'All this stuff … this house, the village, everything … it felt like a dream. Like it wasn't real. It was only when I met you … that I felt alive. You, Ray, you made me feel alive. Even while you were preparing to … die.'

Ray looked at her, his smile gone. 'I don't want to die,' he said quietly. 'But if I do, I don't want to die with any regrets.'

He leaned forwards and kissed her.

As his lips touched hers, a bolt of electricity coursed through her, and in that moment Annie felt certain that the magic her grandfather had spent his life searching for really existed. As the kiss ended and Ray pulled away, she looked up into his eyes.

'I have to go,' he said. 'But if I can … I'll come back.'

26

SECRETS REVEALED

'AREN'T YOU TEMPTED TO JUST SOMETIMES JUMP IN?' Annie said to Mr. Fairbrother, as she sat beside the old man beneath a canvas awning on the lakeside, the lines of their fishing rods disappearing into two holes they had cut in the ice a few metres offshore. A light snow fell around them, pattering gently on the awning like the padding of animal paws. The sun was low in the sky on the other side of the lake, and far around the lake to their right, the lights of Undercastle glittered.

'I fell in once,' Mr. Fairbrother said. 'Not an experience I'm keen to repeat.'

'But, wouldn't it make you feel alive?'

'I feel alive enough already,' Mr. Fairbrother said. 'The ache in the old thighs when I get home from an afternoon of weeding certainly isn't no figment of the imagination.'

Annie was silent for a moment, thinking about Ray, who had departed on the steam train in the morning. Despite her protestations, he had refused to take or give her any contact details. If he couldn't come back, he said, it was better that she not dwell on it. And if he could, she would know.

She had felt like her heart was breaking beneath the thundering wheels of the train.

'You're thinking about that young man, aren't you?'

Annie nodded. 'I'm trying not to, but I can't. It's kind of stupid isn't it? I mean, I barely knew him. There was just something … a connection that I've never felt before.'

'You know, it can come in different ways,' Mr. Fairbrother said. 'Love, I mean. You can know someone for years and it slowly builds up on you, or it can hit you like a bolt of lightning. Will it last? Who knows? I think we all like to think it will, but sometimes it does, sometimes it doesn't. First saw me wife in Preston. She was standing on the other side of a fountain and our eyes met.' He slapped his hands together hard enough to make Annie jump, then grabbed for his fishing rod as it slipped off his knees. 'I thought that was it. I walked round there, asked her if she wanted to get some fish'n'chips, and we were married a month later.' He sighed. 'Didn't last, though. She had a wandering eye. I held things together as long as possible, but in the end I had to let her go. For those first few years though … I wouldn't trade them for owt. And now, it's different. The kids … we're close. You know, they're all coming for Christmas.'

'Really?'

'Yeah, fancy that. Gonna have a right knees up, drink too much sherry, eat more Christmas pudding than the rest of the village combined.'

'That sounds lovely.'

'So try not to get too down about your young man. You had those moments, however brief. If there aren't owt more, hold on to those with every ounce of your strength, because even when they're just memory, they're still there.'

'I think I'm going to….'

Too late, Annie began to sob. Mr. Fairbrother put an arm around her and patted her on the shoulder.

'There, there—oh, feel that! We've got one!'

Annie's fishing line jerked, the rod nearly falling off her knees. She grabbed hold of it, keeping it steady. Then, wearing gloves, Mr. Fairbrother gently lifted the line away from the ice.

'Reet, gently, start winding him in.'

Annie did as she was instructed, and a couple of minutes later a fine salmon broke out of the hole, flapping on the ice.

'Nice one!' Mr. Fairbrother said. 'Reet, that'll do us. Let's get back to the house, see if we can tempt her downstairs out from her cave to cook it up for our tea. Not sure I can handle beans on toast again.'

Back at Stone Spire Hall, they found Isabella in the kitchens, joyfully stirring a vat of baked beans, humming a Christmas song to herself as she turned a wooden spoon with two hands like a witch's enthusiastic young apprentice.

'No sign of Marge again tonight?' Mr. Fairbrother asked.

Isabella shook her head. 'Resting,' she said. Then, leaning her head over on to her shoulder, she gave a chuckle and resumed her stirring.

'Is it worth me trying to talk to her?' Annie said. 'She didn't want to speak to me before, but I suppose I could try again.'

Mr. Fairbrother smirked. 'You could use your authority on her,' he said. 'After all, you're the boss, and if there's something Marge respects more than owt else, it's rules.'

Isabella lifted her hands, made a growling motion, then giggled and grabbed for the wooden spoon before it disappeared into the beans.

'All right,' Annie said. 'I'll give it a try.'

She left them to finish preparing dinner, Mr. Fairbrother muttering something to Isabella about putting the fish in the microwave, then headed up the corridor to where Mrs. Growell had her rooms. She paused outside Mrs. Growell's door, took a deep breath, then gave a sharp knock.

There was a long pause, then finally, a quiet voice said, 'Yes? Who is it?'

'Ah … it's Annie. Ah, Miss Collins.'

The door opened a crack. 'Oh, Mistress. I do apologise. I've been feeling under the weather of late but I hope I can resume my duties in the morning.'

Annie closed her eyes for a moment, then tried to imagine she was refusing someone for a mortgage. 'Mrs. Growell … I demand that you tell me what's going on. It's not like you to behave in this way. If you're sick, you need to let me know. And if you're not … you need to explain yourself.'

She was sweating, but hoping the light in the corridor was too dim for Mrs. Growell to notice. The housekeeper stared at her for a moment, her face tensing, then she gave a curt nod.

'Very well. Please come in.'

Mrs. Growell stepped back from the doorway, holding the door for Annie to enter. Mrs. Growell's suite was smaller than Annie had expected, two small rooms with an en suite bathroom. Barely bigger than a budget hotel room, there was space in one room only for a bed and desk. In the other was a two-seater sofa, a small television, and a bookshelf.

'You live a … ah, frugal life,' Annie said. 'Wouldn't you like a room with a window?'

Mrs. Growell looked at her, eyes widening just enough to show a hint of surprise. 'You mean … move upstairs?'

Annie nodded. 'You don't even have a window down here.'

Mrs. Growell looked down at her feet. 'It was always convenient to be close to the kitchens,' she said. 'And I wasn't one to complain to Lord Collins.'

'About that … what happened the other day? With the suit? Ray didn't mean any harm. He didn't have anything to wear.'

Mrs. Growell nodded again, then went to a bedside table, opened a drawer and took out a slim photo album. She sat down on the bed and set it on her lap. After a moment, Annie sat down beside her.

'I don't have many photographs,' she said. 'As you remember, your grandfather didn't approve of cameras. I suppose I allowed myself a brief rebellion.'

Annie chuckled, thinking it was an attempt at a joke, but Mrs. Growell said nothing. She lifted the album's cover, and to Annie's surprise, the first picture was of a much younger, smiling Mrs. Growell holding a newborn baby in her arms.

'Mrs. Growell … I had no idea.'

Mrs. Growell nodded. 'No one did. A nurse took this picture … the father wasn't present. He didn't know either.'

Annie stared. There was something about the child—

Mrs. Growell turned the page. A baby, drinking from a bottle. A toddler, sitting among a pile of toys. The same toddler, hair much longer, stacking blocks as high as her head.

The page turned. A little girl of pre-school age, standing beside a squatting Mrs. Growell, that all-too-rare smile beaming out of her face. And more, a sense of pride, of achievement, of … love.

And the child, hair tucked behind her ears, had become familiar.

'Is that … Isabella?'

Mrs. Growell nodded. 'Yes.'

'But I thought she was left on the steps of the hall—'

'She was.'

'But the first picture?'

Mrs. Growell nodded. 'That's my secret. It was I who left her there.'

'She's your daughter?'

'Yes.'

'I don't understand….'

Mrs. Growell turned the page again, and this time revealed a photograph which appeared taken professionally. Isabella, around five years old, wore a light blue school jumper, a grey skirt, and a joyful smile. Mrs. Growell, standing on one side, looked dressed up for a ceremony, while on the other side was an older man….

'Is that him? Is that my grandfather?'

Mrs. Growell nodded. The man was handsome in a faded way, an actor past his prime, a sports star with his playing days long behind him.

'It was her first day of school,' Mrs. Growell said. 'I convinced him that we should represent her as parents would. It took some effort to talk him into it, but in the end … he agreed.'

Annie's grandfather had a thin smile on his face, one forced for the camera. Annie gave a little gasp as she recognised the suit he wore as the same one Ray had put on. She looked up at Mrs. Growell.

'That's why you got upset.'

Mrs. Growell nodded. 'After the day Isabella was born, that day was the happiest day of my life. And the memory of it … was almost too great to bear.'

Annie nodded, then immediately frowned. 'But … wait a minute.'

She stared at the photograph. In it, Mrs. Growell looked to be around fifty, Annie's grandfather much older, at least sixty, maybe more. But in their faces, and in Isabella's—

'He was Isabella's father, wasn't he? Oh my god.'

It had happened one night after too much to drink, after Mr. Fairbrother had gone back to his own cottage, leaving Mrs. Growell and Wilfred alone. They had got to talking, and one thing had led to another. Mrs. Growell, who had always harboured a secret admiration for her employer, had hoped it might be the start of something, but Wilfred had immediately withdrawn back into his own private thoughts. Mrs. Growell, saddened, but bound by duty, had slipped neatly back into her housekeeping role and said nothing more about it.

And then she had found out she was pregnant.

Already into her mid-forties, Mrs. Growell had considered all the options available, but in the end the desire to be a mother over anything had won over any other option. However, the fear for what it might mean for her job meant she had to make a few adjustments.

Forever the master of appearances, she began to subtly change her clothing in order to disguise the growing bump, then, when it became too much to hide, she invented a story about a sick relative that needed to be cared for, and took a sabbatical for a few months, moving down south, where she had her baby. Then, upon her return, she sneaked the newborn Isabella back into the house.

To Annie's even greater surprise, it turned out that Diane Jenkins had been in on the secret, slipping into the house through a service door to look after Isabella while Mrs. Growell took care of her housework duties. Eventually, though, Mrs. Growell decided that another plan was needed to bring Isabella's existence out into the open, but in a way that wouldn't jeopardise her position within the household.

Sneaking outside one night before clearing the dinner things away, she left a basket containing a six-month-old Isabella on the doorstep, rang the bell and then waited for events to unfold. Wilfred, by that time living within his search for magic, had been easily fooled. And Mrs. Growell, who managed most of his accounts, had taken care of the necessary paperwork.

'He became her father, without realising he was actually her father, and I became her mother,' she said. 'All the while pretending in front of him that I wasn't actually her mother. In private, however ... I was always her mother.'

'Does Isabella know?'

'She's grown up believing that I was her mother,' she said. 'Your grandfather told her she came from the fairies, but I've told her the truth.'

'And he never realised?'

Mrs. Growell chuckled. 'He was a good man, your grandfather, but he was also an obsessed man. Obsessed with his searches for whatever truths he wanted out of life, and blind to whatever was going on around him.'

Annie puffed out her cheeks and let out a long breath. 'This is hard for me to take in. I mean … it's such a deception.'

Mrs. Growell sighed. 'It was and it wasn't. I wanted to tell him the truth, but he enjoyed the lie more. He thought she was some kind of magical creature, and doted on her as a result. Had he known she was merely his own daughter….'

Annie nodded. 'I see. I have one more question. Mr. Fairbrother said there were no tracks left in the snow, which was one reason Grandfather thought she was delivered by fairies. How did you manage that?'

Mrs. Growell actually chuckled. 'I waited until the storm had died down, then climbed out on to the porch roof through an upstairs window,' she said. 'I used a wire coat hanger on a string to lower Isabella's basket, then I poked the doorbell with one of Mr. Fairbrother's gardening poles.' She chuckled again. 'And people say I'm so unadventurous.'

Annie pointed at the photograph of the three of them together. 'Is this the only one you have of the three of you?'

Mrs. Growell nodded. 'The only one of us as a true family. That day … that was a wonderful day.'

And with that, to Annie's amazement, Mrs. Growell began to cry.

27

CHRISTMAS PREPARATIONS

THE NEXT FEW DAYS PASSED IN A BLUR OF PREPARATIONS, competitions, mince pie production, and bad karaoke evenings. The village council had decided to hold a Christmas bash like no other, so everyone was roped in to help. Annie, technically as head of the council, was supposed to yay or nay each proposal, but everything that the council put to her sounded awesome, so she just told them to decide for themselves, and let her know afterwards if there was tape that needed to be cut or competitions that needed to be judged. She was busier than she had ever been in her life, hurrying from one place to another while attempting to welcome as many tourists as possible and check in on all the staff to make sure they had everything they needed, but in many ways, that was preferable.

Too much time to think, and she would think about Ray.

He had been gone two weeks, and there had been no word. For the first week, she had found herself lingering by the station as the train came in, hoping to see him step down onto the platform, a look of hope on his face. Each time, however, she was left disappointed, and as a week passed, her own hope began to fade. She didn't want to think of him lying in a hospital bed somewhere, or worse, so it helped to keep herself busy. With each day that passed, though, another piece of hope was chipped away. Christmas magic or no Christmas magic, sometimes there was nothing that could be done.

On the 19th, however, on the seven p.m. train, Annie was waiting when Julie, followed closely by her husband Darren and their three children, came bundling off the train. She wrapped her arms around Julie, who whooped with excitement at the sight of the pretty fairy lights shining through the snow that blanketed the station.

'Made it,' Julie gasped. 'Wow, is this it? It's better than I ever imagined. It's truly magical.'

'Where's Father Christmas?' asked her youngest, tugging at Julie's hand. 'I want to see Father Christmas.'

Annie smiled. 'He has a grotto down the street,' she said, pointing at the steps down from the station. 'It's lovely.'

'What about reindeer?' the little girl asked.

'Come on,' Annie said. 'I'll show you. Let's just bring your cases this way and we'll get you up to the house. Then, if you want, we can walk back down and explore. All the paths are lit by Christmas lights and everything's open until ten o'clock right up until New Year.'

'You have taxis?' Julie asked.

Annie shook her head. 'Not exactly. Come on, I'll show you.'

She led them down the platform steps, the kids running ahead, Darren and Julie pulling their cases.

'No way!' came the little girl's cry.

'Taxi?' Mr. Fairbrother said, snapping the reins of an

ornate sleigh sitting at the curb, six reindeer harnessed and ready to pull them up to the house.

'Can I stroke one?' the little girl asked.

'Sure,' Mr. Fairbrother said with a chuckle. 'They're all harmless. Just don't feed them any fudge. Too much sugar is bad for their cholesterol. That one at the front there, Glitter, she's a fiend for the stuff.'

'Talking of fudge,' Darren said, as Mr. Fairbrother climbed out of the sleigh to help them load their cases into a luggage area at the back, 'I heard there's a pretty good shop here....'

Annie grinned and patted her stomach. 'The best I've ever had,' she said.

'Then what are we waiting for?' Darren said. 'Let's get up to the house, get dinner, then get back down for some fudge and a hot chocolate.'

Julie frowned at him. 'What are you? Fourteen?'

Darren grinned. 'It's Christmas. Isn't everyone?'

Out on the ice around the pier, a skating competition was in full swing, the skaters illuminated by a ring of fairy lights, and paper lanterns suspended on wires between poles across the ice. Along the water's edge, a line of barbeques were grilling up tasty salmon caught in the water during an afternoon ice-fishing event, while around the pier, a number of other temporary stalls had been set up, selling everything from toffee apples to knitted Father Christmas tea cosies. The village was about at maximum capacity, with smiling tourists thronging the streets. Two days to go before Christmas, and it was looking like the greatest street party of all time.

Annie stood beside Julie, who was clapping her gloved

hands together in time with the music. Darren had taken the children off on a tour of the Wonder Toy Studios.

'You know, I saw this place on the news the night before we came,' Julie said.

Annie nodded. 'Word has spread fast. We're fully booked right over Christmas. I've just had the village council ask if they can build another hotel for next year.'

'You get to make decisions like that?'

Annie shook her head in disbelief. 'It's a far cry from saying yes or no on a mortgage, isn't it?'

'I bet you can't believe it, can you?'

Annie sighed. 'Not really. But you know—'

'Oh, look, the competition's finished. That means us casuals can have a go.' Julie lifted up a pair of ice-skates. 'Not sure my feet'll still fit into these, but I'll give them a squeeze.'

Annie smiled. 'Good luck.'

She watched a delighted Julie making her way through the crowd towards the ice, where the competition had just ended. Other people were heading down for a spin too. She smiled as a jovial grey-haired lady patted a stern older man on the shoulder. 'Come on, Greg, it'll be fun.'

'I'll break both my legs and then fall through the ice,' the man—who looked like he ought to be a headmaster—moaned. 'And I imagine there are awful things in the water.'

Annie didn't hear the woman's reply as they moved on into the crowd, but a delighted laugh told her what the woman thought.

With everything feeling a little more bittersweet than she might have liked, Annie watched the crowd for a few more minutes, before spotting Diane standing by the barbeques. Giving her a wave, Annie wandered over.

'Hi, not on duty tonight?'

'Got a student holding the fort,' Diane said. 'I've been training a couple up. Got to let them stand on their own two feet eventually, haven't you?'

'I … ah … found out about Mrs. Growell and Isabella.'

Diane lifted an eyebrow. 'Did you now?'

Annie nodded. 'It was quite a surprise. Why didn't you say something?'

'It's not really my place to talk about things like that.'

'But it changes everything, you know. Isabella was my grandfather's daughter. She's my … aunt.'

Diane laughed. 'I don't think you could find one that was more scatty or entertaining. You should be pleased.'

'It's just … weird. And you know, it means—'

'Oh, hang on a sec,' Diane said, holding up a hand. 'That's one of my staff. What's he doing down here?'

A young man was making his way through the crowd towards them. He wore a Christmas hat, but otherwise looked distraught.

'What's up?'

'We're out of chocolate sauce,' the student said. 'I don't know where the other ones are.'

Diane glanced at Annie and rolled her eyes. 'Just a minute, I'm coming,' she said to the student. 'See you later, Annie. Enjoy!'

Annie raised a hand. 'I'll try.'

As Diane followed the student back towards the pancake house, Annie sighed again. Everyone was having a great time—which was good, of course—but she couldn't shake off a feeling of regret.

She glanced at her watch. Seven forty-five. The last train of the day would be coming in at eight. As she did every time, Annie headed up to the station, taking a seat on the platform. As the train pulled in with a whistle and a puff of steam, she looked up expectantly, and as she always did, she scanned the smiling faces as they burst out of the train doors, hoping against hope that Ray might be among them. But, like every time she had waited, the passengers passed through the doors to the station, or down the steps out on to the street, and soon the platform was empty.

And Ray wasn't there.

Annie stood up and headed back to the house, her party spirit evaporating with her hopes. She found Mrs. Growell in the entrance hall, vacuuming the floor. They gave each other a curt nod, before Annie announced she was heading up to bed.

'Are you all right, dear? I mean, Mistress?'

'I'm fine,' Annie said. 'Merry Christmas.'

Mrs. Growell smiled. 'And to you. Would you like breakfast at the usual time tomorrow, or would you prefer to lie in a while? It's Christmas Eve, after all.'

Annie smiled. 'The usual time will be fine.'

'As you wish, Mistress. Oh, by the way, Mr. Fairbrother was looking for you.'

'Really?'

'Yes. Something about tomorrow evening's Christmas parade. I last saw him in the armoury, polishing the swords.'

'Okay, thanks. I'll go and find him.'

There was no sign of Mr. Fairbrother in the armoury, but after wandering through a few of the rooms, Annie eventually found him in her grandfather's art gallery, wiping the dust off the frames of the paintings. He looked up when she entered and clapped his hands together.

'Ah, Mistress, there you are.'

'You were looking for me, Les?'

Mr. Fairbrother gave a frantic nod. 'Aye, aye. It's of the most utmost importance. Can you give me a couple of minutes of your time?'

'Sure.'

'Reet, follow me.'

He led her out of the art gallery and through the house to a back entrance that led out on to a courtyard. Since Annie had arrived it had been covered in snow, but now Mr. Fairbrother went up to a narrow door Annie hadn't noticed before, and pulled a key out of his pocket.

'Where does this go?'

Mr. Fairbrother grinned. 'Your grandfather's workshop.'

'His … what?'

'There's a main door out there, where the garden slopes down towards the tarn. Sorry, never got around to showing you. It were top secret, he always said.'

He opened the door and switched on a light to reveal a concrete staircase leading down. Without waiting to see if she followed, Mr. Fairbrother started down, his footsteps echoing on the steps, suggesting a large chamber at the bottom. After a brief moment of indecision, Annie followed after, closing the door behind her to keep out the snow.

The air was cold and smelled of oil and dust. Annie put her hand over her mouth as she reached the bottom of the stairs. Mr. Fairbrother switched on another light and she found herself in a huge underground garage, the walls lined with tools, workbenches, desks. And in the centre, something huge was covered with a cloth tarpaulin.

'You know your grandfather was a bit of an inventor, don't you?' Mr. Fairbrother said. 'Well, this were his masterpiece. He never got around to using it. Said he'd wait 'til the village opened. Of course, we know what happened there.'

He walked up to the hidden object and began to drag the tarpaulin away. Annie gasped as a shining gold and silver sleigh was revealed, all ornate metal frames and pipes. Large enough to seat a dozen people, it was the size of a small bus.

'He … built this?'

Mr. Fairbrother nodded. 'The whole thing. By hand, out of recycled material. I mean, I helped him a bit, mostly just passing him things to weld together.' He chuckled. 'It has a few bells and whistles.' He tapped a box on the side. 'This is the music player. And those pipes on the back, they release fireworks. And at the back there, if you press a button, there's an outboard motor hidden in that there gold box. You see, it can also float. You just have to press a button on the dash and the runners open out into floats, allowing it to move on water. Of course, you'd have to unharness the reindeer first.'

'Reindeer? Reindeer can pull this thing? It's huge.'

'Eighteen,' Mr. Fairbrother said. 'Your grandfather, he weren't a man to do anything by halves.'

'I can see that.'

'It was intended to be the centrepiece of the Christmas Eve parade. Of course, the parade never actually happened. Tomorrow will be the first one, and the council guys were asking me about it … you see, your grandfather kept his cards close to his old chest, and no one is sure this thing even exists.'

'But it does.'

'And it would be a shame not to use it, would it not?'

'Most definitely.'

Mr. Fairbrother cupped his hands together and gave a sheepish grin. 'However, as I'm sure you're aware … Lord Wilf isn't with us anymore. Therefore … there's a bit of a vacancy in an important position. I know they's got that guy works down the grotto, but he's just for the kids and don't know his way round a sleigh. Lord Wilf was supposed to be the main guy, and I was only ever going to be an understudy, but you know, in the Master's absence … if you want, I'd be happy to step up.'

Annie couldn't help but grin. 'I think you'd make a wonderful Father Christmas.'

Mr. Fairbrother's eyes lit up. 'Then I've got the job?'

'It's all yours. I can't wait.'

Mr. Fairbrother started to laugh. 'This is going to be the best Christmas ever. Me kids arrive in the morning. Don't tell them, please. I want it to be a surprise.'

'Aren't they all grown up?'

Mr. Fairbrother shrugged. 'Ah, but it's Christmas, isn't it? No one ever really grows up at Christmas, do they?'

28

SUCCESSES AND GIFTS

Isabella was tugging on her sleeve. 'This morning,' she said. 'Come, come.'

Mrs. Growell was down in the kitchens, washing up the breakfast things. Mr. Fairbrother had already gone down to the station to meet his children off the early train, while Julie and her family had taken breakfast in the dining hall and then headed straight down to the village for a snowman competition.

'All right, I'm coming,' Annie said. 'Let me get my coat.'

Isabella was enthusiastic even for her, practically running back to the forest, with Annie struggling to keep up as she trudged through snow that was almost knee-deep. How Isabella managed almost to float across the snow like a fairy perhaps led some credence to her grandfather's assumption of her heritage, but it was far more likely due to a lower intake of fudge and mince pies. Huffing as she climbed up through the trees, Annie patted her stomach and promised to go on a diet in the New Year.

By the time she reached the top of the rise to find a

crisp and clear snow-covered landscape waiting for her in all its breathtaking majesty, she had hardly any breath left anyway. Isabella was waiting at the crest of the hill, a bag at her feet and her little musical instrument in her hands.

'Throw, throw,' she said, pointing at the bag. 'This time for sure.'

'Did you make some adjustments?' Annie asked.

Isabella lifted her free hand and made an OK gesture. 'Bingo,' she said.

'All right, let's try.'

Annie took the clockwork bird out of the bag and held it gently in her hands. It looked exactly the same as before: an intricate, delicate thing, so easily broken. She couldn't even begin to imagine how the girl had made it, but now saw in Isabella's eyes Mrs. Growell's quiet determination, which, when mixed with her grandfather's belief in the magic of the world, had created something that was almost pure creativity in human form. Isabella, Annie realised, not Stone Spire Hall nor even Undercastle, was her grandfather's true legacy, one of which he had died unaware.

'Okay, I'm ready when you are,' Annie said.

'Fly!' Isabella cried, throwing her hands into the air and giggling at the same time.

Annie took this as her cue. She tossed the bird into the sky, immediately wincing as it caught and spun on the wind, angling into a nosedive. Then, however, a miracle happened.

Instead of crashing down into the snow, it spread its wings inches above the ground, its beak barely brushing the snow before it soared back into the air. Isabella was tapping frantically on her musical pipe, and the bird was responding, its wings flapping in time with the tune as it dipped and rose on the wind like a kite cut free from its tether and taking on a life of its own.

Laughing, Isabella began to make it do tricks, the bird swooping low over their heads, soaring up into the air and then executing neat rolls and loops. By the time Isabella brought it down to land neatly on Annie's forearm, Annie had begun to think of it not as a toy at all, but as a living, breathing creature.

She stared as Isabella came over and took the bird gently in her hands then lowered it back into the bag.

'That was amazing,' Annie said. 'What on earth did you do?'

Isabella met her eyes and smiled. 'Nothing,' she said. 'I … believed.'

Her eyes twinkled as the sun broke from behind a cloud, and in that moment Annie felt sure that there was real magic in this place. Then, Isabella turned away, picked up her bag, and headed for the path back down the hill.

'Hungry?' she called back over her shoulder. 'Mid-morning snack?'

Annie smiled. 'Let's go,' she said.

Mrs. Growell was wiping down the cupboards in the entrance hall when Annie returned from the hill. After taking off her boots, gloves, and coat, Annie rubbed her hands together in front of the fire for a few minutes, watching Mrs. Growell clean, building up her courage for the conversation that was coming.

'Um, Margaret?' she said, steeling herself. 'Have you got a minute?'

Mrs. Growell paused and looked up. 'A minute? Yes, Mistress. I can spare a minute.'

'I wanted to give you something,' Annie said, taking an envelope out of her jeans pocket. 'It's kind of a Christmas present.'

Mrs. Growell frowned. 'Mistress, it's really not necessary.'

'Oh, I think it is. Here.' She held out the envelope for Mrs. Growell to take. 'You can open it now, if you like. Then I can explain.'

Mrs. Growell frowned again, then tore open the envelope and pulled out a plastic file containing several sheets of paper stapled together. 'What's this?' she said, looking up.

'It's the deeds to the house,' Annie said. 'I spoke to Grandfather's lawyer yesterday and he faxed something over to the house last night. I've thought about this a lot, and I believe that my grandfather should never have given this place to me. He hadn't updated his will for many years, and he was unaware that Isabella was even his daughter. By rights, this place should go to her. However, in light of her being something of a fruitcake,'—here even Mrs. Growell let out a brief chuckle—'I feel it's better for the house and its estate if you be named legal custodian until such time that you deem Isabella capable of taking over. It's you, Margaret, who is the real heart and soul of this place. Not me, not my grandfather, not anyone else. You are Stone Spire Hall's beating heart, and you always have been.'

Mrs. Growell stared at the file, blinking over and over as though unable to believe what she was seeing. Her mouth opened and closed a couple of times before she could finally summon the strength to speak.

'I … I don't know what to say. Mistress … I'm not sure I can accept this. I don't know how to run a manor house.'

'You've been doing it very well for the last thirty or forty years,' Annie said. 'I'm sure you'll be fine.'

'But what about all your grandfather's businesses? And what about you?'

Annie shrugged. 'Well, I have a few requests, if I may. I believe it was my grandfather's wish that Undercastle be open to the public, and I'd like it to stay that way. And I think it would be right that such a wonderful place be shared with the world. Therefore, I'd like to oversee a program to bring school parties and children from disadvantaged backgrounds here on trips, perhaps even for study holidays. I don't know the logistics of it all, but I don't want to see this place left off the map like it has been all these years. It's too … magical.'

'I see. I'm sure we can come to some arrangement.'

'And I'd like to keep one of the empty houses in the village, if you don't mind. I noticed a few were unoccupied.'

'Of course.'

'All of these requests are down to your good grace, of course. I've signed over everything to you. I have no rights nor legal influence over anything anymore. But … you know, it is Christmas.'

'Mistress, you can't!'

'I can. Believe me, I've thought about this a lot. However, I have one last request, if I may.'

'Anything, Mistress.'

'I'd like to ask you for a job.'

'A job? I think I have the house under control already.'

'I meant in a wider sense. Something like tour manager, or operations coordinator, or something with a wordy name that makes me feel important.'

'Well, if that's what you want. But … Mistress Annie, how can you give this up?'

Annie smiled. 'Because being the lady of the manor and all that, it's not me. It's never been me. When all this happened to me a few weeks ago, I was at the lowest ebb I think I've ever been in my life, but coming here, meeting all of you, discovering this new world I never even knew about … it was like a dream, and for a while I went with it. But now I think it's time to wake up, and come back down to earth. I don't want to sit on top of a mountain telling people what to do. I'd rather be at the bottom of the mountain, enjoying the view. Ideally with a glass of wine in my hand.'

'Wouldn't we all,' Mrs. Growell said, looking at the ground. Then, looking up at Annie, she said, 'I really can't accept this. I think you're being impetuous again.' She rolled her eyes. 'It was one of his traits. Isabella has it in spades, and it looks like a little filtered down to you as well. However, as a practical person, I am prepared to reach a compromise, if this is really what you want.'

'What kind of compromise?'

'At all costs, I believe that what your grandfather created here should be … protected.' She reached up and wiped away a tear. 'My dear, dear Wilfred … his memory is so sacred to me. However, he was a man with a vision, with a gift he wanted to share with the world. He died before he was able to share it, but now … you're right. Now is the time.' She sighed. 'But I'm an old woman, and running such an operation isn't for me. I'm a housekeeper, not an estate manager. I'm happy to be involved, if that's what you want, but I think that everything should be shared between yourself, myself, Mr. Fairbrother and Isabella.' She smiled. 'As a team.'

Annie smiled. 'Great, if that's what you want. I'm sure Grandfather's lawyers would jump at the chance to take a little more of his money to draw up something official. Only if you're sure that's what you want.'

'It is, Mistress.'

Annie nodded. 'Then here's to the future.' She reached up a hand for a high five, but Mrs. Growell just shook her head.

'Please don't attempt such bizarre gestures with me,' she said. 'But I appreciate the thought. Would you like a cup of tea?' She sighed. 'There's far too much sugar around at this time of the year.'

Annie smiled again. 'I'd love one,' she said.

29

MERRY CHRISTMAS

DOWN IN THE VILLAGE SQUARE, A BIZARRE CHRISTMAS cake relay was in progress. Children carrying large wooden spoons had to race across the square, scoop up mounds of fruitcake and cream from what had begun as the biggest Christmas cake Annie had ever seen, then rush back across the square and dump it into a bowl set in front of their seated parents, who had to finish the bowl before the next load arrived. Any who failed dropped out of the race.

Annie, watching from the sidelines with Mr. Fairbrother on one side and Mrs. Growell on the other, clapped her hands as Davvie Sprinkle-Toes, in full elf regalia, raised a hand over the last empty bowl, and the two winning parents gave a grim smile and a wave to the cheering crowd.

'What a hideous sight,' Mrs. Growell said. 'Such a terrible waste of food.'

'Come on, Marge, it's Christmas,' Mr. Fairbrother said. 'Can I interest you in a glass of mulled wine?'

'I'll think about it.'

'Don't think too long. There won't be any left in half an hour.'

Mrs. Growell sighed. 'All right. Half of a small glass.'

'Only one for you too, Les,' Annie said. 'Remember you're driving the sleigh tonight.'

Mr. Fairbrother turned to a tall young man standing beside him. 'Ah, not to worry,' he said. 'I've convinced my lad Mike here and your friend's husband Darren to do the driving for me. I'll just be bringing the ho ho ho's.'

'It was the idea of wearing forest green leggings that sold me,' Mike said. 'Who could say no?'

'Well, it'll be spectacular, that's for sure,' Annie said.

'Are you coming for a glass?' Mr. Fairbrother asked as the group started to move through the crowd.

Annie glanced at her watch, then shook her head. 'Maybe later. I have something I have to do first.'

Mr. Fairbrother held her eyes for a moment, then nodded. 'Well, we'll see you later.'

'Okay.'

Annie watched them go for a moment, then turned and hurried up the street to the train station. The next train was due in a couple of minutes. There would only be one other today, the last before Christmas.

She was on the platform just as the train puffed and whistled into the station. The funnel let out one last blast of steam, then with a hiss of hydraulics, the train settled, and the carriage doors opened. People bounced out, into the arms of waiting friends, or the circles of guesthouse reps and lodge couriers, or just to stand in wonder at the view from the platform down the gentle slope of the Christmas village by the lake. Annie, standing expectantly, waited until the last new arrival had cleared off the platform, leaving it empty. From a side door, Willy Whistle appeared, a broom in hand, ready to clear away the trampled snow left in the wake of the departed new arrivals. Annie caught his eyes for a moment, and he gave her a sad smile before resuming his work.

No sign of Ray. Annie, who had let the unstoppable hope of Undercastle inflate her, slowly began to slide into despair. Still, there was one more train. Maybe, just maybe.

She was still standing at the end of the platform when the evening's departing guests began to arrive. Some hugged new friends and old, some laughed, some shed tears. Annie, feeling empty inside, watched as people climbed into the carriages and gave last goodbyes, before the train belched a puff of steam, Billy blew a whistle, and the little locomotive chugged out of the station, its carriages bumping and rocking in its wake.

'Every train for the last week,' Billy said, and Annie looked up, giving a little shake of her head to find him standing right in front of her.

'I'm sorry, I was in a bit of a daze there,' she said.

'I'm afraid I haven't seen him,' Billy said. 'The man from the waiting room, I mean.'

'How did you…?'

'Word travels fast.' He gave her a kind smile. 'Don't give up hope. There's still one more train. Why don't you go and watch the live Christmas karaoke for a bit. If nothing else, it'll cheer you up.'

Annie couldn't help but smile. 'I just might,' she said. 'The last train's at seven thirty, right?'

'That's right. Then none again until the twenty-seventh. It's been a wonderful season. I've never seen so many happy people. It's thanks to you, you know. Lord Wilf was never going to open this place to the public. I thought I was going to go crazy sweeping the platform every day, seeing the train just sat there. Go and enjoy yourself. You deserve it.'

Annie nodded. 'I'll try. Seven-thirty, right?'

'Go on!' Billy said with a chuckle. 'I'll have a hot chocolate ready so at least your hands won't get cold.'

'Thanks.'

She headed back down into the village. To her stunned surprise, Mrs. Growell had taken the stage in the village square and was crooning her way through a note perfect version of White Christmas, while Les, one hand around Isabella's shoulders and another around the shoulders of a woman who, from her uncanny resemblance to the old caretaker was clearly his daughter, laughed and sang boisterously along. Sitting at a sound desk at the stage side, every few notes Bunty Glitterbottom turned the microphone up a notch, until Annie was sure Mrs. Growell could be heard in Lancaster.

One by one, customers and staff got up on the stage to sing raucous renditions of classic Christmas songs. Mr. Fairbrother, like some precious unearthed fossil, did a stunning version of Slade's Merry Christmas Everybody, while Isabella, complete with a prancing, strutting stage performance, pulled off a pretty competent version of Mariah Carey's All I Want for Christmas is You, getting pretty close to the high notes, but not quite high enough to stop several people wincing and clapping hands over their ears.

Just as Mr. Fairbrother put his hand up for another song, Julie appeared out of the crowd and gave his arm a shake.

'There you are,' she said. 'The boys were looking for you. It's time.'

'Time for—*oh*,' Mr. Fairbrother said. 'Huh, I was enjoying myself so much I quite forgot the time.'

'Luckily your elves didn't. Let's go.'

'Do you need some help?' Annie asked, but Julie shook her head.

'Amazing the things you learn about people, isn't it? I had no idea Darren did work experience at Bristol Zoo when he was a teenager. He was like an old hand harnessing up those reindeer. I felt almost jealous.'

'Are you sure that wasn't the elf costume?'

Julie grinned. 'He does look rather fetching. Even if it did split down one leg so it looked a bit like a skirt.' She howled with laughter, patted Annie on the arm, and said, 'But don't worry, we covered it over with a bit of wrapping paper. Right. Wait here. We'll be back in a bit, once we've got the old timer into his costume.'

Annie waved goodbye as Julie led Mr. Fairbrother back through the crowd. She tried to concentrate on the festivities, but it was impossible, and she found herself checking her watch constantly, ticking down the seconds to the last train of the day. Long before half past seven rolled around, she was sitting on a bench on the platform, waiting as the train arrived.

No Ray.

As the platform emptied, she shook her head. It was a romantic thing, that was all. He could just as easily arrive on a train on the twenty-seventh or twenty-eighth. It wouldn't matter, as long as he came.

She refused to think about the alternative, that he might never come, that by now he could already … already….

'There you are,' Billy Whistle said, sitting down beside Annie and passing her a steaming cup of hot chocolate. 'I didn't notice you sitting all the way up here. You know, the station's officially closed now, so I'm going to have to order that you go and enjoy yourself, even if, you know, you are technically my boss.'

Annie smiled. 'It's okay.'

'Did you know, one of the ancient festivals on which Christmas is based was Saturnalia, a Roman festival?'

Annie shook her head. 'No, I didn't know that.'

'It was a kind of midwinter knees up, lasting ten days or so. And one of the things that was popular was a role reversal. Servants assumed the role of masters, masters became servants. So, in the spirit of that ancient festival, I, your staff member, command you, my boss, to go and enjoy Christmas Eve.'

'Technically I just gave Undercastle to Mrs. Growell,' Annie said.

'Huh. Well, I don't think anyone would dare tell her what to do,' Billy said. 'Come on, give me five minutes to lock up, then we'll go down together. Isn't Father Christmas coming at eight o'clock?'

Annie nodded. 'That's right.'

'Well, we don't want to miss that, do we?'

'No, we don't.'

'All right then.'

She waited while he closed and locked up the station building, then together they headed down into the village square. The road that led to Stone Spire Hall was lined with people, and the square was packed. Annie didn't think she'd ever seen so many happy faces, nor so many Christmas hats. The air was filled with the scents of delicious Christmas food, and the tingle of piped Christmas music permeated the crowd.

Suddenly a bell began to ring. The crowd hushed, and a light appeared up in the forest behind the village. Something bright and illuminated appeared through the trees. Annie stared as a line of reindeer appeared, their harnesses lit by fairy lights, followed by a massive gleaming sleigh. Two elves held the reins, another stood on the top beside a huge sack. Between the two elves at the front sat a jovial, rotund Father Christmas, white-gloved hands waving to the crowds, 'ho ho hos' bellowing out of a speaker hidden somewhere on the sleigh's rear.

'Merry Christmas!' he roared, and the crowd cheered in response. 'Merry Christmas, everyone! On this fine night in Undercastle, I'd like to wish you a wonderful Christmas and a very happy new year!'

'The old fool's overdoing it a bit,' Mrs. Growell, who had appeared next to Annie, muttered under her breath. Then, with a sudden smile, she added, 'But he does look magnificent, doesn't he?'

'Where's Isabella?' Annie asked, looking around, as the sleigh pulled into the square and came to a stop.

Mrs. Growell smiled. 'Over there. That's the girl Wilfred believed in. And I suppose, in a way, he was right.'

Annie squinted through the glittering lights. Isabella was sitting on the back rail of the sleigh, dressed as a fairy. She waved to the crowd, then pulled something out from under her dress. Annie stared as she recognised the musical instrument she had used up on the top of the fell.

'Welcome, all!' Father Christmas roared, and as though on cue, the elf on top of the sleigh pulled open the top of the sack. Isabella began to tap on her instrument, and seven beautiful, silver clockwork birds flew out of the sack and began to duck and weave in the air overhead to stunned gasps from the crowd. Mrs. Growell grabbed hold of Annie's arm, almost pulling her over, and when Annie turned to the older woman, she saw tears in Mrs. Growell's eyes.

'That's my girl,' the housekeeper sobbed. 'That's my little girl.'

'And now it's present time!' Father Christmas roared. 'Come one, come all!'

The crowd began to approach the sleigh, mostly parents waving their children forward. As the birds wheeled and dipped overhead, the elves passed gifts out of the sack down to Father Christmas who handed them out, shook hands, ruffled hair, and bellowed 'ho ho ho' at every available opportunity. Annie, hanging back with Mrs. Growell, waiting until almost everyone had received something, then slowly approached, as the surrounding festivities began to resume.

'Ah, there you are, dear,' Father Christmas said to Annie. 'I have something very special for you.'

Annie smiled. 'You don't need to give me anything,' she said. 'That was just perfect.'

'Ah, but there's perfect, and then there's Christmas perfect,' Father Christmas said, giving her a wink. Then, glancing over his shoulder, he called, 'Lad, come over here.'

Annie glanced up at the sleigh, wondering why he was calling Darren or Mike, then remembered with a sudden jerk of her heart that there was a third elf. As the man turned, and she saw a familiar smiling face beneath the green peaked cap, she felt her knees falter.

'Quick, Marge, catch her,' Father Christmas said.

Mrs. Growell's arms were like iron. Annie let the housekeeper hold her until she could regain her senses, then slowly she stood up, reaching out for Ray, pulling him close.

'You're here,' she said. 'I waited. Every train, I waited. I didn't think you'd come back. I thought you were....'

'I'm alive,' he said, stroking snowflakes out of her hair. 'I'm in remission. I knew it. There's magic in this place. Magic that's been set free. It saved me once, and it's saving me now. There's a long way to go, a lot of pain to face … but I'm going to make it. I know I am.'

Annie could barely bring herself to speak. 'The train…?'

'It was fully booked,' Ray said. 'I had to catch a bus, but it broke down. By the time we'd all made it through the snow to the house, we were barely in time.'

'We?'

Ray shrugged. 'I'm afraid there are thirty school children bound for Carlisle staying in your house tonight. I hope you don't mind? Les said it would be fine, but he said I should ask. In any case, he needed another elf, and who wouldn't want to try on one of these suits? Aren't they neat?'

Annie could only smile and shake her head. 'You look ridiculous. What happens next? Where do we go from here?'

'Tomorrow is tomorrow,' Ray said. 'Why worry about tomorrow, when we can enjoy today? It's a beautiful evening. Wonderful food, wonderful people, wonderful company. Let's enjoy it, and tomorrow we'll see what happens.' He took her hand. 'I don't know about you, but I've never been swimming on Christmas Day. Would you like to join me?'

Annie smiled. 'I think I can handle that,' she said. 'I want something first, though. She reached out and plucked a sprig of holly off the sleigh, then bent down and picked up some snow, which she sprinkled over the top. 'There, that looks a bit like mistletoe, doesn't it?'

'Close enough,' Ray said.

Annie smiled. 'Then you know what to do. Merry Christmas, Ray.'

'Merry Christmas, Annie,' he said, leaning forward. He closed his eyes, and with a contented, relieved sigh, she closed hers too.

The tinkle of Christmas music filled the air.

Somewhere nearby, an announcer called for a second round of Christmas karaoke. Snow had begun to fall, and as Annie held Ray close, she felt the gentle chill of snowflakes landing on her skin.

Sometimes, she thought with a smile, it was worth believing in a little Christmas magic, just in case.

Merry Christmas

Acknowledgements

Many thanks goes to Elizabeth Mackey for the cover, Jenny Avery for your endless wisdom, Paige for the editorial stuff, and also to my eternal muses Jenny Twist and John Daulton, whose words of encouragement got me where I am today, more than ten years after the journey started.

Lastly, but certainly not least, many thanks goes to my wonderful Patreon supporters:

Carl Rod, Rosemary Kenny, Jane Ornelas, Ron, Betty Martin, Gail Beth Le Vine, Anja Peerdeman, Sharon Kenneson, Jennie Brown, Leigh McEwan, Amaranth Dawe, Janet Hodgson, and Katherine Crispin

and to everyone's who's bought me a coffee recently:

Spyke, Lindsay, Rosemary, Mariane, Denise, Janet, Christine, and a couple of anonymous readers

Your support means a great deal. Thank you so much!

For more information:
www.amillionmilesfromanywhere.net

Printed in Great Britain
by Amazon

28557649R00130